Christmas in Evergreen Point

Angela Flowers

CHAPTER 1

It was almost dark when Stella pulled to a stop in front of the brick building sporting a battered sign that read 'Store'. Well, she'd wanted a small, out of the way town. Here it was.

The 'town' consisted of two—maybe three streets. The municipal part anyway. She hadn't paid much attention to the residential side on her way in because it was getting late and she had been on the road for hours. She was tired. She was hungry. She was … well, pretty cranky.

"Almost there," she muttered to herself as she dragged herself out of the vehicle. Stretching, she groaned as a gust of wind nearly blew her back into the car.

There was a bite to the air that suggested a temperature drop was on its way. That was just fine. She was looking forward to a nice fire and a bottle of wine.

Let the cold come.

As she approached the store, she saw that its name was actually 'Bo's General Store'.

"Better than just 'Store'," she told herself before pulling the door open.

The warming scents of cinnamon, cloves, chocolate, and butter filled her nostrils.

"Well, hello there," an older gentleman with a gray, scruffy beard and hair greeted her from behind the counter. "You must be Mrs. Lowe."

Ignoring the pang in her chest, she said, "Just Stella, please."

"Okay. Stella then. Welcome to Evergreen Point."

"Thanks," she sighed as she looked around.

She'd never actually been in a real general store before but it looked like every one she'd ever seen on TV. Rows of everything from cereal to canned goods to light hardware filled the room. There was even a small display of linens in the back corner. Buckets of candy tempted customers near the register. There was a bakery display along the back wall filled with sugary delights.

"If you give me just a few minutes, I'll get your cold items packed up for you," the man said. "Name's Howard, by the way, but friends call me Howie."

"Not Bo?"

"That was my grandfather."

Of course it was, Stella thought. This place has probably been in the family for generations.

"So, what brings you to town?" Howie asked as he began removing items from the refrigerator, checking them off a list, and placing them in a sturdy cardboard box. "We don't usually get a lot of visitors this time of year."

"I need some time to myself," Stella said, fighting the urge to hug herself. "I figured a cabin in the woods was a good place for that."

"It sure is," Howie agreed. "Okay, I think this is all of your order." He set the box on the counter next to two more boxes and a couple of brown paper bags. "I'll take them to the car for you."

"Thank you. I can help."

She grabbed the bags and followed him outside. While she situated the bags and boxes in her backseat, Howie went back inside for the remaining boxes. Once everything was loaded, she offered him a tip but he politely declined.

"No need for that around here." Howie waved a dismissive hand. "We like to keep things friendly."

"Oh, okay," she said. "Well, thank you for your help. I should get going before it gets too dark."

"That's probably a good idea. Feels like a storm is brewing."

On cue, another chilly gust kicked up the leaves and dirt around their feet. Stella shivered and pulled her coat tightly around her.

"Be careful out there. The road to the lake is dark and winding," Howie said. "It was nice meeting you, Stella. I'm here if you need anything. There should be a list of local phone numbers on the refrigerator at the cabin."

"Thank you."

She got back into her car while he returned to the warmth of his store. She started the car and headed for her final destination of the day. According to the navigation app, she had about ten minutes to go.

Howie was right; the narrow road to the cabin was shrouded by trees that even though bare of leaves, still managed to block the waning light of the setting sun.

Stella took her time, slowing down at the bends in the snaking road, as gravel crunched beneath the tires. With each passing second, she could feel the tension draining from her body. Finally, the trees parted and she came to a fork that split the road into a loop around the lake. A large sign of cabin addresses told her to turn right, so she did.

She passed several small driveways with their corresponding houses lurking beyond. She thought of them as lurking because they were all dark and empty. Not too many people picked lakeshore getaways in November in New Hampshire. It wasn't exactly good swimming weather.

"And then there was light," she said as she spotted her rental, its windows lit up in warm welcome.

She pulled into the driveway of her cabin and cut the ignition. It was bigger than she needed with four bedrooms, but she wanted to be on the water and it was the only one available. Not too many people rented out their homes during the winter. At least she would have plenty of the quiet she was seeking.

She got out of the car and opened the back door to retrieve the box of cold food. She would take the food and other necessities inside first. Then, she would bring her clothes and other belongings in.

As she started up the steps, the front door swung open. Surprised, she almost dropped her box.

"Welcome to Evergreen Point," a deep voice greeted her.

Stella took in the sight of the large man dressed in jeans and a dark green flannel shirt and almost snorted.

How cliché.

"Hi," she said. "I, uh, wasn't expecting a welcoming committee."

He chuckled. "Just me, I'm afraid." He came forward, reaching for the box. "Here, let me."

"That's okay. I've got it, Mister …"

"Call me Caleb."

Nodding as she passed him on her way inside, she said, "Nice to meet you, Caleb. I'm Stella Lowe."

"I'll help you with the rest of your things before the storm hits."

She started to protest but when she looked back over her shoulder, she saw that he was already gone.

Okay then.

She set the box on the kitchen counter and looked around the cabin. The first floor was completely open, except for the bathroom, of course. There was a fire going in the large stone fireplace. A big, plush L-shaped sectional sofa sat in front of it. An eating area off to the right of the living space was home to a large table and chairs. Beyond that was what she assumed was a large set of doors hidden by thick, thermal curtains to block the cold. Tomorrow she would open them to enjoy the full view of the lake, but for now she would enjoy the cozy warmth they provided.

Caleb returned, setting two more boxes on the counter, and told her if she opened the trunk, he'd help her with her things.

"Thank you, but I can handle everything from here," she replied.

"I'm sure you can, but the wind is picking up. It will be faster if we work together. Unless you enjoy toting luggage in the pouring rain."

He had a point.

She smiled. "Okay."

Together they finished unloading the car. He insisted on carrying her suitcases upstairs to the master bedroom, while she put her groceries away.

When he came back downstairs, Stella thanked him again for his help and assured him she would be good from here. He frowned and rubbed his stubble-covered chin.

"I don't want to keep you out in the storm," she insisted.

"It's not a problem. I'm in the cabin next door."

She stiffened. "Oh, I thought you were from the rental company."

"I guess you could say that. Unofficially anyway." When she just stared at him, he explained, "Since I own the cabin next door, I often help out. My sister runs the rental company."

"Ah, so you're obligated to help out."

He chuckled again. "We help each other out around here whenever help's needed."

"Small town thing?"

His grin widened. "Small town thing."

"Well, thanks again."

"You're welcome," he said as he pointed at the fridge. "My number is posted there if you need anything. Have a nice night."

"You too."

Once he was gone, she sighed. She was beginning to think he would never leave. Good grief. She'd always heard people were super friendly in small towns like these. It was true, she guessed.

"Not here to make friends," she muttered.

No, she was here to get away from people.

She went upstairs and put sheets on the king-size bed. After that was done, she unpacked her clothes, hanging some in the closet and tucking the rest away in the chest of drawers. Then she unpacked and organized her toiletries in the en suite.

"Now you and I are going to get acquainted," she told the claw foot tub. "But first, a glass of wine."

She went back downstairs to the kitchen and found a glass and corkscrew. She'd brought a few bottles of her favorite red with her, and in a few days, a case should arrive at the general store. She opened a bottle, poured a glass, and took it upstairs to enjoy a nice, hot bubble bath.

The wind howled outside, followed by the rushing sound of rain as the storm finally arrived. With a contented sigh, Stella lowered herself into the warm water. She rested her head back against the porcelain and closed her eyes. She took several slow, deep breaths, inhaling the rising steam and releasing the lingering tension in her body.

This was the break her mind, body, and soul needed.

CHAPTER 2

The next morning, Stella awoke to the sound of rain pounding the windows. That was fine by her; she would enjoy a relaxing day inside. Downstairs, she boiled water for her French press. Once she had her coffee steeping, she went to the wall of thermal curtains at the back of the house. Even though the view was a dreary, rainy one, she couldn't help but gasp when she pulled the curtains aside. The sight of the seemingly endless lake stretching before her brought a sense of peace. There was something restorative about being close to the water. She couldn't wait for the weather to clear, so she could get outside and take full advantage of its therapeutic effects.

Once her coffee was ready, Stella left the curtains open and took her mug into the living area and set it on the low coffee table. She tended the fire before settling onto the sofa to watch the flames dance.

As her mind wandered, a sudden thud at her door startled her. Heart in her throat, she vaulted to her feet, nearly knocking over her coffee in the process.

"What the hell?" she gasped as she stared at the door.

The only sound now was the crackling of the fire in the stone fireplace. Taking a deep, steadying breath, she crept quietly across the cabin. When she got to the door, she paused.

Should she open it? Or should she go back to the sofa and pretend it never happened? Maybe it hadn't. She was so lost in her own thoughts that she very well could have imagined it. It wouldn't be the first time.

"This is ridiculous," she muttered.

It's not like there were a lot of people here. The wind. That's what it was. The wind had probably blown something onto the porch. Or maybe a bird had flown into the door. The thought made her flinch. If it was a bird, it might be injured. She should check.

Thump, thump, thump.

This time, the sound was followed by a soft scratching sound.

Oh, no. It *was* an animal. Now the only question was what *kind* of animal?

She swallowed hard as she debated on opening the door. Wait, the window! She moved to the window and drew back the edge of the heavy curtain. The sight of Caleb walking up her steps sent another startled jolt through her.

What was he doing here *again*?

He knocked on the door, and she pulled it open.

"Good morning," he said. "Sorry to bother you."

Was he really?

A low whine had her looking down at her feet, where a black lab sat looking up at her expectantly. Its tail began to thump against the porch planks once more and its tongue lolled sideways out of its mouth.

"Well, hello," Stella said, dropping into a welcoming crouch.

"Name's Boomer," Caleb said. "I guess he wanted to meet you."

Reaching out to scratch his ears, Stella said, "Hi, Boomer. Aren't you a handsome fella?"

She was rewarded with a generous lick to her arm, making her laugh.

"Come on, Boomer," Caleb said. "You've said hello. Let's leave her be now."

Still petting the dog, Stella looked up at him. He was dressed in another flannel shirt, blue this time, and jeans. His dark hair dripped with rain and his eyes, she noticed, were a deep, comforting chocolate brown. Much like the dog's.

"Would you like a cup of coffee?" she heard herself asking.

Caleb shook his head. "No, thank you. I'm going to run into town. Need me to pick up anything for you?"

"No, thank you. I think I'm all set."

After all, she'd only just arrived the night before with a car full of provisions.

"Okay. Boomer, come!"

The dog gave her one last lick before turning and bounding down the steps. Caleb gave a little wave and then the two of them were heading back across the yard to the cabin next door.

Once they were gone, Stella went back inside. Feeling slightly chilled now, she returned to her spot in front of the warm fire and drank the rest of her coffee. Then she went into the kitchen to fix herself some breakfast. Eggs and toast were easy enough. Quick, too.

After she ate and washed up her dishes, she poured herself another cup of coffee. She grabbed her tablet, connected it to the cabin's Wi-Fi, and returned to the sofa. She pulled a thick blanket over her lap and settled in to browse her social media.

All of her friends were busy preparing for the upcoming holidays. Meal planning, gift buying, and house cleaning. Thanksgiving was in two weeks. After that, Christmas would come zooming right along behind it. She flinched at the thought.

This would be her second Christmas without her late husband, Dale. Her heart clenched as his smiling face invaded her thoughts. Christmas was his favorite holiday and he always went all out with the decorations not only inside, but outside as well. He would start at the beginning of November and turn their house into a winter wonderland.

Although she'd never been a huge fan of the holiday, she would always help him. Starting out, she would be, as Dale liked to tease her, a bit of a Grinch, but it didn't take long for Dale's contagious kid-like joy to change her outlook.

Now he was gone, taking what little holiday spirit she had with him.

A tear escaped from the corner of her eye and trickled down her cheek. She hastily wiped it away. Taking a deep breath, she closed the app on her tablet to banish the painful holiday reminders. If only it were that easy to block out all of the memories in her mind.

Her phone beeped at her from the kitchen counter but she ignored it. It was probably a text from her son, Noah. He wasn't too happy about her plans this year.

Neither of her children were.

"Who goes to the lake in the winter?" he'd said when she'd told him about her plans. "You can't just run away, Mom. It's *Christmas*."

"Exactly," she'd replied.

Last year she'd stuck around for him and his sister, June, even though what she'd really wanted was to run away. This year she was taking the break she desperately needed from the holiday season. Her children didn't understand. While her heart needed a break, theirs needed the comfort of tradition. They saw the holiday as way of staying connected to their father, which Stella understood completely, but it was that connection that she needed to get away from this year. It was too painful.

Dale was gone. No matter what they did, how they carried on his traditions, that wouldn't change. They would never see his smile again. Hear his joyous laugh. She would never feel the comforting strength of his arms around her again. Every twinkling light, strand of garland, and Christmas lyric was a stabbing reminder of that. Over and over, without reprieve.

So, this year she was avoiding all of it in a rental cabin by the lake. Secluded and without the heartbreaking reminders pummeling her every time she turned around.

Shoving the sad thoughts away, she opened the reading app on her tablet and found a nice, simple cozy mystery to escape into.

CHAPTER 3

Stella read well into the afternoon, stopping only to make a quick sandwich for lunch. Around three o'clock, she finally stopped to rest her eyes and ended up taking a quick nap on the sofa.

When she woke up, she stretched and then went into the kitchen to start on dinner. The weather outside was still gray and dreary, so she decided to throw together a pot of beef stew. It was hearty and comforting. Plus, she would have leftovers to freeze for the next several weeks.

She turned on the small television to have some background noise while she cut the beef into chunks and browned it. Then she added broth and got to work peeling and chopping potatoes and other vegetables to add with the stew meat.

Once the stew was on, she decided some fresh air was in order. She bundled up in her heavy coat and boots before stepping out into the damp air. She closed her eyes and took a deep breath. Then, she trotted down the steps and set out to walk along the shore.

While peaceful, the silence was also a little nerve wracking, highlighting the fact that she was indeed very much alone out here. The houses around the lake were all dark and foreboding. If something happened to her out here, no one would know. There would be no one to help her.

Telling herself she was being silly because nothing was going to happen to her, she continued meandering along the uneven ground of the lakeshore. She made it halfway down one side of the lake before her stomach began to growl in earnest.

"Gosh, this is beautiful," she said out loud to herself.

Even in its current gloomy state, the lake and its surroundings comforted and energized her. Feeling awake—and cold—she sighed loudly and turned back towards her cabin. The cozy glow from the windows beckoned her, promising warmth. She picked up her pace.

Next door, Caleb's cabin was also lit up, a reminder that she wasn't *completely* alone out here. She supposed that was a good thing. You know, in case something *did* happen and she needed assistance.

To her surprise, she saw that he was sitting outside on the back porch. Boomer was lying at his feet. Was he watching her?

An uneasy tingle snaked along her skin at the thought. She shook it off, telling herself once again that she was being silly. Caleb wasn't spying on her; he was simply enjoying some fresh air just as she was doing.

When she approached their cabins, Boomer gave an excited bark before bounding down the steps in her direction. She couldn't help but smile as the dog danced around her legs in welcome. After giving him a quick pat, she continued her trek back with Boomer guiding the way.

"He likes you," Caleb called out.

"I think so," she said. "I like him, too."

Her declaration brought a smile to his face. "It's hard not to like him. He makes it so easy."

"He is a good dog."

Even though Boomer was excited to see her, he hadn't jumped on her. He was very polite.

"Did you have a nice walk?" Caleb asked.

"I did." She paused in the back of her cabin. "I know it's not the best walking weather, but I needed some fresh air after being inside all day."

"Cabin fever already, huh?"

She gave a small laugh. "Maybe."

"When you're used to going all the time, slowing down is an adjustment."

"Isn't that the truth?" she agreed. "Well, I should get inside and check on my stew." Her manners got the best of her and she asked, "Would you like to join me? I made a big pot."

Caleb smiled wider, making the corners of his eyes crinkle. "Thanks, but I have dinner plans in town in about an hour."

Of course he did. He was probably meeting his girlfriend or maybe even his wife. Her eyes automatically went to his hand. No ring. So, girlfriend then.

Not that she was interested in him like that. She didn't come here for romance. In fact, that was the last thing she needed in her life right now.

"Okay then," she said. "Enjoy your dinner."

As she started up her steps, he said, "You too. Come on, Boomer. Back over here."

It was only then that she realized the dog was sitting beside her back door. She laughed. "I can watch him while you're gone if you'd like."

"You sure?"

"I don't mind at all. Honestly, it will be nice to have some company."

"Okay. I'll be by later to pick him up."

She opened her door and Boomer ran inside straight into the kitchen, where he sat down in front of the stove.

"And here I thought you wanted to visit with me," Stella chided. "You smelled that from outside, didn't you?"

He wagged his tail, thumping the floor in exuberance. She took off her coat and boots and joined him in the kitchen to check on the stew. She gave it a stir, inhaling the savory scent of beef and herbs in the process.

She glanced at the clock and then said, "It's got about forty more minutes to go, Boomer. Then I'll be sure to share some with you. How's that sound?"

As if he understood, the dog thumped his tail again before following her into the living area. She added another log to the fire and stoked it a bit before sitting on the sofa. Ever the gentleman, Boomer sat on the floor and gave a soft 'woof'.

"Look at you. So polite." She patted the cushion next to her. "Come on up."

Boomer gave an excited bark this time before jumping onto the sofa and curling up next to her. He set his head in her lap, so she could pet him while they waited for dinner to finish cooking.

She flipped through the TV channels and finally settled on an old action film to help pass the time. The movie was already halfway through but she didn't mind.

About forty-five minutes later, she went into the kitchen and ladled stew into two bowls. Then she cut two pieces of bread. She handed one to Boomer, who was sitting patiently at her feet.

"Now, you'll have to wait for the stew to cool a bit," she told him. "You don't want to burn your mouth."

She chuckled at herself for talking to the dog as if her were a human as she carried her bowl to the small table. She poured a glass of wine and then slathered butter on her bread. When she finally dug into the steaming bowl of hearty stew, she groaned in appreciation.

The warmth of the meaty broth spread through her body and she sighed. This was the perfect meal after a damp and chilly walk. She was glad she'd put it on to cook before she left.

While she ate, Boomer laid beside her chair, but didn't beg. Instead, he slept peacefully, as if he understood he needed to wait for his helping to cool. Perhaps he had understood when she'd explained it to him. Not only did he seem well-mannered, but he seemed highly intelligent as well.

When Stella was done, she set Boomer's bowl down on the floor. Then she washed her own bowl and glass. The rest of the stew would have to cool before she could put it away.

Finished with his portion, Boomer licked his lips as he looked up at her.

"Ah, not a big vegetable fan, huh?" she said when she saw that he'd left most of them behind in the bowl. "That's okay."

She dumped them in the trash and then washed his bowl. By that time, he had reclaimed his spot on the sofa and was fast asleep. Smiling, she joined him. It was nice to have some company after all.

CHAPTER 4

The ringing of her phone woke Stella up. It took her a minute before she remembered where she was. Next to her, Boomer yawned loudly and looked at her questioningly. She tossed the blanket aside and went to the kitchen for her phone.

"Hello?"

"Stella?"

"Yes, this is she."

"Hey, it's Caleb. I hope you don't mind that I got your number from my dad."

She frowned. "Your dad?"

"Howie from the store."

Of course they were related.

"Anyway," Caleb continued. "I was thinking about staying in town tonight. You can take Boomer over to the house and let him inside. The door's unlocked."

"Or I can just keep him here for the night," she said.

"That too. Only if you don't mind though. I don't want him to be a bother. He'll be just fine on his own at home."

Shaking her head, she glanced at the snoring dog on the sofa. "He's quite comfortable here, I think. I don't mind keeping him for the night."

Chuckling, Caleb said, "Let me guess. He's knocked out in front of the fire and snoring his butt off."

"You know him well."

"I do. Well, thank you. I'm sorry to do this."

"Caleb, it's not a problem. He's been a perfect gentleman all evening."

They said goodbye and then Stella called out to Boomer, who reluctantly slid off of the sofa in a long stretch.

"Come on, buddy," she said. "It's been a couple of hours since you've been out."

She grabbed her coat, slipped on her boots, and walked out onto the porch to wait while the dog ran out into the grass. He wasted no time and immediately ran back to the house.

"You're such a good boy," she murmured as she rubbed behind his ears.

Boomer returned to his spot on the sofa, while she shed her coat and toed off her boots. Then she poured herself another glass of wine before joining him.

"How about a movie?" she asked the dog. He replied with a thump of his tail. "I'll take that as a yes. Hmm, let's see."

She found the Netflix app on the TV and entered her login information. Then she idly browsed the movies until she found the most recently released rom-com and pressed play.

When the movie was over, she went upstairs to bed. Boomer stayed right on her heels and eventually curled up next to her in the big bed. She wasn't sure if he was allowed on the bed normally, but she didn't have the heart to kick him out. He looked so comfortable, and on the plus side, he offered extra warmth.

The next morning Caleb picked up Boomer right after breakfast. Stella was surprised at the feeling of sadness that came over her as she watched him go. The cabin also seemed bigger without Boomer in it.

Since the weather was nicer today, she took her second cup of coffee outside to sit on the back porch overlooking the lake. The air was still cold, so she put on her coat and took a blanket outside with her. Bundled up in the lounge chair, she sipped her hot coffee and watched the sunlight play on top of the water.

This was exactly what she had wanted when she booked this place. Peace and quiet. While the rest of the country was rushing around and preparing for Thanksgiving and Christmas, she was here enjoying the outdoors stress-free.

Was she going to miss seeing her kids for the holiday? Absolutely. But she wasn't going to miss all the hustle and bustle or the stories about Dale. She got it. Even grown, the children missed their father. They needed to rehash the memories over and over again. But she needed a break. This past year she'd been so caught up in making sure Noah and June were adjusting okay that she didn't make it a priority to find time for herself to grieve. That's what this trip was about.

While watching the ripples created by the light breeze on the top of the water, Stella opened the door in her mind that held her memories of Dale at bay. Grief washed over her, as if the breeze had carried it to her. Instead of trying to stamp it down as she usually did, she embraced it. When she felt the tickle of tears trickling down her cheeks, she didn't bother to wipe them away.

"Boy, I sure do miss you," she whispered hoarsely. "I still can't believe you're gone."

A small gust of wind picked up, sending dried leaves twirling across the porch, as if Dale were answering her. She liked to think that he was sending her a message. Telling her he missed her, too. That this whole trip wasn't as crazy as Noah and June thought it was.

Dale would understand. Somehow, he had always known what she needed and he tried to give it to her. Of course, she did the same for him, but she always felt like he understood her on a deeper level than she did him. No matter how hard she tried, she couldn't find the capability to anticipate his needs as well as he did hers. Even so, they worked.

Their marriage wasn't perfect by any means. Whose was? But she liked to think they fought less than other couples. Sure, they had disagreements occasionally, but she could probably count on one hand the number of times they'd outright yelled at one another.

She smiled. They were best friends. True best friends. Not too many couples could say that. A lot did, but it wasn't true, not in the truest sense of the moniker.

And now she had to figure out how to navigate life without him. Without her best friend. Her husband. Her companion.

Of course, she didn't *need* a man to take care of her. She was perfectly capable of taking charge of her own life. She always had. She'd just had Dale's support as back up for the past twenty odd years. That was what she was going to miss. Sure, she had Noah and June, but it just wasn't the same.

Her children couldn't provide the companionship she would miss and she didn't expect them to. But she was going to miss having that one person to share not just the big parts of life, but the little ones as well. Sitting on the sofa together, her feet in his lap, while they both read. Cooking dinner together and dancing to music while watching over the food cooking on the stove. Enjoying their morning cup of coffee with each other.

She wasn't sure how long she sat there lost in her memories but her coffee mug was empty and her stomach reminded her that she had skipped breakfast this morning. Feeling more at peace than she had in a while, Stella rose from her comfy cocoon and went back inside.

She heated up some leftover stew. After she ate, she decided to go for another walk, a longer one this time since the weather was much nicer. She took her time ambling along the shore, stopping every so often to skip rocks along the mirror-surface of the lake.

As expected, most of the homes were closed up for the season. She found herself wondering what the people who owned these homes were like. Were they younger or older? Did they use the houses as family vacation homes or did they rent them out for most of the summer season?

She envisioned children running and playing along the shore. Jumping from the docks into the refreshing water in the heat of the summer, while their parents and grandparents watched from their chairs dotting the shoreline.

When she turned back to go back to her cabin, she found herself wondering about Caleb. He said he lived here. Did that mean he stayed here at the lake full-time? Or was he just here because she had rented the cabin next door? She felt a little twinge in her chest at the thought. What if her presence was keeping him from his family? His job?

Well, that was a silly thought, she told herself. He probably worked in town, which meant he could easily drive ten minutes or so to go to work. Last night he'd stayed in town. He'd probably wanted to spend time with his family.

As their houses came into view, she wondered if he was inside his house right now or was he off at work somewhere? What did he do for a living anyway? She snorted. He probably ran the local hardware store or something. After all, his dad owned the general store and his sister owned the house rental company.

As if she'd conjured him up, Caleb rounded the corner of the house with Boomer right behind him. He was carrying something, but Stella couldn't tell what it was because she was still too far away. He raised his arms and she realized it was an ax. He brought it down and a loud *thunk!* echoed across the water.

24

Stella stopped and watched in disbelief. He was actually chopping firewood. The man really was a walking small town cliché. A small giggle wiggled its way up her throat, and she covered her mouth with a gloved hand.

Recovered from the small shock, Stella resumed walking. Hearing her, Boomer raised his head, looking in her direction, and gave a bark. Caleb turned in her direction as well, shading his eyes with his hand. Then he raised it in a friendly wave.

Smiling, she waved back. Boomer was already racing towards her. When he reached her, his body was in full wag mode, his rump bumping against her legs, almost knocking her over. Laughing, she crouched down to scratch him behind both ears.

"Hey there, buddy," she said.

Then she continued on her way with her new walking companion. When she got to her rental property, she called out a greeting to Caleb, who had steadily chopped wood as she approached.

"Hey," he answered, pausing to wipe his brow. "I'll bring over some more firewood in a few minutes."

"More?" She looked at small lean-to that housed rows of chopped logs.

"Yeah. There's another storm system brewing. Need to make sure we both have plenty of firewood in case the power goes out."

She'd never even considered the possibility. "Does that happen a lot?"

He shrugged. "Depends on the season. I like to be well prepared if it does go out though. Better to be over prepared than under."

She supposed that made sense.

"We probably don't have anything to worry about," Caleb added. "But I would hate for you to run out."

"Thank you. That's very considerate."

"You're welcome. I have to admit, I'm not used to having guests this time of year, so I'm probably worrying too much. Even if we don't need the wood for this particular storm, it will come in handy at some point. Did you enjoy your walk?"

"I did. It was much nicer than yesterday's."

He nodded and looked down at the ax in his hands. Clearly, she was interfering with his work, so she excused herself and headed inside. It was only then that she realized she was out on this lake with a strange man who had an ax.

"Oh, stop it," she told herself as she removed her coat and hung it up. "You've seen too many movies."

She went upstairs and indulged in another bubble bath. While she soaked, she thought about the impending winter season. She hadn't really given any consideration to the possibility of being snowed in with no power. Did she have the right provisions for such a situation? She had stew in the freezer but what about other food? She supposed she should go into town and stock up on some canned goods just in case. While she was there, she could check on her wine order, too.

CHAPTER 5

When Stella got to town, she took her time becoming acquainted with it. Though small, there was a decent selection of shops, some boutiques even. She found a beautiful, fluffy robe that she had to have. The old, worn one she'd brought with her was proving to be inadequate and she knew once the weather turned colder, it would pretty much be pointless.

She wandered from store to store, introducing herself to all of the friendly shop owners. To say the experience was nice would be an understatement. She saved the general store for last, of course.

"Good afternoon, Stella," Howie greeted her from behind the counter. "Are you psychic?"

She frowned. "What do you mean?"

"Your wine order just came in."

"Oh! That's great news, considering there's a storm coming. Speaking of which, I realized that I didn't have a good supply of food for the storm. You know, in case the power goes out."

He nodded. "Ah, so it would be canned goods and other nonperishables you're after today? In addition to your wine, I mean."

"Yes. I have some stew in the freezer but I think I should expand my options."

"I agree. It's also good that you're coming in now before the mad rush. I try to keep an eye on the weather forecast, so I can order extra supplies, but it's hard to predict who needs what and how much around here."

"I can imagine."

"Of course there's always the big chain stores in neighboring cities."

"Oh, I would much rather give you the business."

Not to mention avoiding the mass displays of holiday décor.

"I thank you for that." He pointed across the store as his phone began to ring. "You'll find what you're looking for in that area over there."

"Thanks." She left him to his phone call, grabbed a basket, and headed for the section he'd suggested.

By the time her basket was full, the door opened and a woman swept inside. She was carrying a huge basket covered with a red gingham cloth. The scents wafting from it filled the store and made Stella's mouth water instantly.

As the woman headed to the bakery case, Howie introduced her as his sister, Darlene. She owned the bakery down the street but also kept his case stocked for those who didn't want to make a separate trip down the road.

"It's lovely to meet you," Stella told her as she watched the woman unload her basket. "Gosh, that all smells wonderful."

Smiling, Darlene said proudly, "I have cookies—chocolate chip, snickerdoodle, oatmeal raisin, and lemon crème—and some fresh baked breads—zucchini and banana."

"Oh, my goodness. That all sounds amazing. I'll take some of those snickerdoodle cookies and some of that zucchini bread off your hands."

"Of course, dear!"

Howie appeared at her side and began wrapping up Stella's selections. "Stella here is renting the Anderson's place for the next several weeks."

The woman's eyes rounded but she quickly covered her surprise with a smile. "Winter is an interesting choice for a lake vacation. May I ask what brings you here?"

"Oh, I just needed to get away from the hustle and bustle of everyday life."

"During the holidays?" When Howie loudly cleared his throat, she quickly amended her question. "Where are you from?"

"Massachusetts."

"Not too far then?"

"No."

A momentary pause bloomed between them before Darlene asked the dreaded question, "So, will your family be spending Christmas at the lake with you?"

"Um, no," Stella said tightly. "It will be just me."

"Oh." She shared a look with her brother, who shook his head. "Thanksgiving, too?"

Continuing to smile, Stella said, "Yes, just me."

"Oh."

Howie smiled and held out a paper bag with her baked goods inside. "Here you go, Stella."

"Thank you. I think I've got all I need for a bit." She nodded at Darlene. "It was nice to meet you."

As she headed to the register counter, Stella tried to ignore the murmured whispers between the siblings. She knew most people wouldn't understand her need to be alone during the holidays, even if she did explain her circumstances, so she couldn't hold their reactions against them.

Howie left his sister and returned to the register to ring up Stella's purchases. She could tell he was bothered by his sister's prying, so she went out of her way to try to make him comfortable.

"When I left, Caleb was chopping wood. He told me about the possible storm system and got me thinking about what I'd do if the electricity goes out."

"Ah, yes. Caleb likes to be prepared."

"So he said."

"You shouldn't be too worried though. As long as you've got plenty of firewood and food you'll be just fine. Of course, you won't be able to watch television and the like. If worse comes to worse, Caleb has a generator."

"He didn't tell me that."

"Probably didn't want to add to your worry." He smiled. "He told me Boomer has taken a liking to you."

She laughed. "Yes, he has, but I'm sure that isn't a surprise. He probably likes everybody he meets."

"You're right about that. But Caleb seems to think Boomer has taken quite a shine to you and you to him."

"He's a great dog. So polite. He doesn't like to eat his vegetables though."

"What?"

While she told him about the stew, Darlene joined them and they both laughed.

"Isn't that just like a man," Darlene said, her eyes shining with laughter. "Meat and bread."

"And potatoes," Stella added. "He picked those out as well."

"Well, I'll be," Howie said.

"I should get going before it gets too dark," Stella said. "I'll see you guys around."

She loaded her bags into the car and then was on her way back to the cabin. She was glad she'd decided to come into town. While the solitude of the cabin was nice, it did feel good to connect with people. Howie was so easy going, she was comfortable talking to him. She imagined he was giving his sister a piece of his mind about her prying questions right now. Stella hoped he wasn't being too hard on her. Really, Darlene's questions hadn't been overly intrusive.

By the time Stella arrived back at the cabin, the sun was setting. As she unloaded her purchases, she began to think about what to cook for dinner. She decided a nice meatloaf and some mashed potatoes sounded good. The stew she'd eaten for lunch was long gone, as her stomach reminded her with a growl.

After she put her groceries away, she started on dinner. While the meatloaf was baking and the potatoes were boiling in the pot, she carried her other purchases upstairs. Along with the robe, she'd splurged on some goat milk soap and lotion. According to the lady at the boutique, they were made at a local goat farm not too far way. Stella had always heard that goat's milk was great for the skin, so she was excited to try them.

She returned downstairs and finished cooking. After she ate, she separated the leftovers and put them in the freezer. Then she got the fire going again and settled in front of it with her tablet. She read for a little while before finally turning on a TV series she was currently watching.

It was a peaceful night after a great day of exploring, and it wasn't long before she fell asleep right there in the living room.

CHAPTER 6

The weather was still nice when she awoke the next morning, so after breakfast she headed out for her walk. To her surprise, she found Caleb and Boomer waiting for her beside the lake.

"Good morning," Caleb said. "I was wondering if you would mind if I joined you this morning. With this storm coming, I figured I should get outside while I can."

She smiled as they began walking. "Sure. How long do they think this storm is going to last? A couple of days?"

"At least. If we lose power, it might take a couple more to get it back."

Oh boy. Now that she was faced with the possibility of being alone in a strange place in the dark, she was getting nervous.

As if he'd read her mind, Caleb said, "Don't worry. Based on what I've seen, it looks like it will blow through fairly quickly but you never know with these nor'easters."

"Are you an amateur weatherman?"

He chuckled. "I guess you could say that. Experience has taught me a thing or two when it comes to the weather here on the lake."

"I bet. Your dad said you have a generator?"

He glanced at her with a small frown. "I didn't tell you that?"

"No, you didn't mention it."

"Sorry about that. Don't worry, I'll share if need be."

"I think I should be okay. I stocked up on some nonperishables, and I have leftovers in the freezer, too."

Stopping to pick up a stick and throw it for Boomer to chase, Caleb said, "I don't think you have too much to worry about with this storm." He smiled as Boomer came racing back with the stick in his mouth. "Good boy." He took the stick, tossed it again, and looked at her as he resumed walking. "I'm right next door if you need anything."

This time Boomer brought the stick to her, so she paused long enough to throw it for him. He took off after it with a happy bark, making her smile. A small gust of wind blew over them, making her hair dance around her face.

"You can feel it in the air," Caleb said. "It's coming."

"Should we head back?"

He nodded. "I need to tie down the furniture on the back deck in case the wind gets really bad."

"Oh. I didn't think about that."

She usually had Noah around to help her prep for storms at home, so she didn't know the best way to go about securing outdoor furniture, especially when she wasn't sure where to find the necessary supplies.

"Don't worry," Caleb assured her. "I'll take care of yours as well."

"Thanks."

They turned together and headed back to their houses. She went inside to pour two hot mugs of coffee before going out onto the back deck. Caleb made quick work of strapping the furniture in place. He gratefully accepted the steaming mug of coffee.

"Would you like to come inside?" Stella asked. "The wind is really starting to pick up."

"No, thanks." He emptied his mug. "I need to get some more stuff done before the storm arrives."

"Okay."

He handed her the empty mug before whistling for Boomer, who darted across the yard to follow him home. Stella took the mugs inside and tidied the kitchen, while making sure to take final stock of her storm supplies. Then she went around and made sure all the windows were locked and the drapes drawn tightly to ward off any drafts. She plugged in her tablet, her phone, and her power block for back up. When she was done, she turned on the TV to check the latest weather report on The Weather Channel.

"Oh!" She exclaimed to herself when the guy on the television mentioned fire wood. "Fire wood!"

Her eyes raced to the rack by the fireplace and she frowned. Was it enough? According to both Caleb and the weatherman on TV, the storm would blow through in two days, but what if it stalled out? And what if the power went out for longer than that? Knowing she was probably being paranoid, she went outside and brought in a few more logs just to be on the safe side.

She heard the sound of tires crunching gravel and went to the window. Caleb's truck pulled up under the carport next door. She took comfort in knowing that at least she wouldn't be out here all by herself. She should probably let her kids know about the impending storm and that she was fully prepared and safe.

After the necessary calls were made, Stella checked outside. It was overcast now, with the clouds darkening by the second. The wind had picked up in a steady howl. She decided to settle on the sofa and watch TV for a bit while she still had electricity.

By dinnertime, rain lashed the windows and the wind howled against the cabin. Inside, Stella was nice and cozy in front of the fire.

It's not so bad, she thought. She was warm and dry. Alone, but comfortable. And besides, Caleb was right next door if she needed anything.

CHAPTER 7

The power managed to stay on throughout the night, for which Stella was grateful. Her nerves kept her awake most of the night as the rain pelted the cabin and the wind howled through the trees. She was pretty sure she'd heard a branch or two snap. This morning she was happy to note that the storm had weakened and now all that remained was a steady rain with the occasional wind gust. Nothing like during the night though.

She went into the kitchen and made coffee. Tired and grumpy, she opted for a reheated slice of zucchini bread instead of cooking. Then she figured what the hell and heated a snickerdoodle cookie too. After all, she was on vacation.

Once she'd eaten and cleaned up, she poured herself a luxurious second cup of coffee and carried it to the sofa. She turned on the TV for some background noise and tended the fire, adding a couple of logs and stoking it until the flames grew strong again. Then she curled up on the sofa with a blanket. As she sipped her coffee, she sent texts to Noah and June letting them know that she hadn't lost power and the storm was on its way out. They were relieved, of course.

Her phone surprised her when it chirped to life in her hand.

"Hello?"

"Hey, there Stella. It's Howie. I hope you don't mind that I got your number off of your order. I just wanted to check and see if you made it through the storm okay."

Well, wasn't that just lovely?

"Why, I'm just fine," she said. "The electricity is still on and I'm tucked in on the sofa in front of the fire. Thank you so much for checking in."

"It's no problem. I know Caleb is right next door, but I wanted to check on you anyway."

"I appreciate that."

"Well, I won't keep you on the phone. Stay cozy today."

"Thank you. You as well."

She smiled as she hung up. It was comforting to know people cared.

After finding an old sitcom on the TV, she burrowed under the blanket and drifted off to sleep. She slept for an hour and when she woke up, she felt more rested and ready to tackle some baking. What better way to spend a dreary, rainy day?

She decided bread sounded good and got started preparing the dough. Once it was proofing, she decided to make a pumpkin roll next. Before long the air in the cabin was filled with the scents of pumpkin and spices and yeast from the rising bread dough. Stella found herself humming as she prepared the cream cheese filling for the roll. Baking never failed to raise her spirits.

Once the pumpkin roll was finished, she checked her dough and found it had risen nicely, so she put the loaf in to bake. Her stomach growled loudly, making her look at the clock. It was well past lunch time, so she made herself a quick sandwich and ate it at the table while she waited for the bread to bake.

By the time her sandwich was gone, it was time to remove the bread. She inhaled deeply as she set the loaf on the counter.

"Perfect," she said to herself.

While the bread cooled, she cleaned up the kitchen and then returned to the sofa. She found her tablet and decided to read for a little while. She'd barely finished the first paragraph when a knock sounded at her door.

When she opened it, Caleb smiled at her. Rivulets of water ran down his rain coat onto the stoop.

"Oh, my goodness!" she gasped. "Let me get a towel."

"Thanks, but there's no need. I just wanted to check in with you." His nostrils flared. "It smells like you've been keeping yourself busy."

"Yes, I've been baking. Not only does it pass the time but I find it soothing as well. Are you sure you don't want to come in? I have fresh bread and I can put on some coffee. Or tea if you'd rather."

"I don't want to intrude."

"Are you kidding? You wouldn't be intruding at all." She stepped back and ushered him inside. "Come on in. Would you prefer coffee or tea?"

"Coffee would be great."

She disappeared upstairs briefly to get a towel. He gladly accepted it and dried his hair after removing his coat and hanging it on a hook by the door. He also slipped his boots off and left them on the rug before following her into the kitchen, where he took a seat and watched her get the coffee going and slice some of the warm bread.

"This just came out of the oven not too long ago," she said, setting a plate in front of him. "I also made a pumpkin roll but it's still setting in the freezer."

"My, you have been busy." He slathered butter on the bread and took a bite. His eyes fell shut and he groaned. "That's so good."

She smiled. "I'm glad you like it."

"It's comforting, especially on a day like today."

"Yes, it is." She took a bite of her own slice before pouring them both a mug of hot coffee. "Here you go. You must be freezing from the rain."

"I'm used to it, so it's not too bad. So, you like to bake."

She nodded. "I do. I enjoy cooking, too. I find creating in the kitchen relaxing."

"You sound like my aunt. She loves to bake, too."

"I'm assuming you're referring to Darlene."

His eyebrows jumped on his forehead. "You've already met her?"

"Yes, she came into the store yesterday when I was there. She's very kind. I even bought some of her zucchini bread and cookies. Oh! Would you like one? They're Snickerdoodle."

He chuckled. "You love to bake, and you're obviously good at it, and yet you still bought my aunt's baked goods?"

Shrugging a shoulder, she replied, "I like to support others. Plus, sometimes it's nice to eat someone else's baking for a change."

"You're a nice person."

She laughed. "Thank you. Why do you sound so surprised?"

He blushed. "I'm sorry. I didn't mean to. It's just that you surprise me. You're different than most city folk that visit here."

She wasn't sure how to take that. She was fairly certain he meant it as a compliment but it unsettled her a little bit. Arching a brow, she said, "City folk, huh?"

"You're from the city, right?"

"Yes, I suppose I am."

"See?" He took a drink of his coffee. "I'm not wrong."

"I guess not. Although you are a tad judgmental."

He snorted. "I just call things like I see them."

Stella decided to let the comment go and took a drink of her own coffee, relishing its warmth.

"Thank you for the bread and coffee," Caleb said as he rose. "This was a nice break, but I should get back. I need to finish what I'm working on."

"Oh? Are you doing some home improvement project?"

"Nah." He shook his head. "Just work."

"You work from home?"

"Most of the time." He went to the door and shrugged into his coat. "Sometimes I'm required to travel or go into the city."

"That's nice. I mean, being able to work from home like that. So, do you live next door full time then?"

"I do. It's another perk of being able to work from home. Anyway, thanks again."

And then he slipped out the door and was gone, leaving her staring after him and wondering why he seemed to be avoiding the topic of his job. Most people would have offered up the title of their job without her having to pry it from them.

So, he worked from home and occasionally had to travel and go into the office. Well, these days he could be doing anything. There were so many jobs that can be done remotely. It was probably something as boring to her as computer programming or data entry. Or maybe he was one of those remote customer service people. The thought made her laugh. Caleb didn't have the right personality for that job.

Shrugging, she cleared their dishes and cleaned up the kitchen. When she glanced out the window above the sink, she saw that it was barely sprinkling now. The storm was almost gone, which was good. That meant she could resume her walk tomorrow.

But for now, she would continue to enjoy the solitude. Although Caleb's brief visit had been … something. She wasn't sure she would call it nice. After all, he'd insulted her and then taken off the second she started asking him questions.

"Weird," she muttered. "That's what it was."

Shaking her head, she turned her attention back to her tablet and the rom-com she was reading.

CHAPTER 8

The days flew by and before Stella knew it, Thanksgiving was almost here. She'd established a good daily routine that included lots of walking, when the weather permitted, of course. There had only been two days of hard rain that prevented her from walking. She didn't let a little drizzle or misty rain stop her. To her delight, Boomer had started joining her.

She barely saw Caleb and when she did, it was in quick passing. He pretty much stayed inside his cabin. That or he would leave in his truck and stay gone for hours. She could only assume he was working but she hadn't asked. Since he was respecting her need for privacy, she wanted to return the favor.

So, when there was a sudden knock at her door the afternoon before Thanksgiving, she was surprised. Although, given the upcoming holiday, she probably shouldn't have been.

When she opened the door, Caleb offered her a wide smile as Boomer pushed his way inside. "Hey," he said. "Sorry to intrude, but I've been given a mission."

Kneeling to pet the dog, she looked up at him. "A mission?"

"Yes, so please don't shoot the messenger."

She chuckled as she straightened. "Okay."

"My aunt insisted that I invite you to Thanksgiving tomorrow."

How had she not seen this coming?

As if he sensed her discomfort, Caleb added, "I told her you probably had your own plans but she wouldn't hear it. For some reason she's worried that you're going to sit here alone all day tomorrow."

Which was exactly what she was planning on doing.

"Look, Caleb, I really appreciate the offer," she began. "I do."

Raising his eyebrows, he said, "You *were* planning on being by yourself tomorrow."

"Sort of. I was planning on visiting my kids via Zoom."

He cringed as he said, "If my aunt finds out I let you sit here by yourself on Thanksgiving, she's going to kill me."

"Why? I'm no one's responsibility."

Not anymore.

"Stella, please don't make me tell her you're going to be alone on Thanksgiving."

Giving an incredulous laugh, she stepped back to let him come inside out of the cold. "Just tell her I told you that I already have plans."

"You mean lie?"

"It's not a lie. Not exactly."

He looked around the cabin, silently noting that Boomer had made himself right at home on the sofa. "I tried to tell Aunt Darlene that you came here for some peace and quiet. I'll be the first to tell you that our family get-togethers are *not* quiet."

44

"Most of them aren't," she said.

"If I tell her you declined, she might just show up on your doorstep. I'm not kidding. So maybe you could, you know, come by, eat, and then leave. Or just come for dessert."

She sighed. And then how would she explain to Noah and June that she could spend the holiday with strangers but not with them? June, especially, would be devastated. She looked forward to cooking for the family every year.

"Thanks, but I still have to say no," Stella said.

"Nooo," Caleb groaned. "If you refuse, they all might show up on *my* doorstep tomorrow and try to coerce you into joining us. Please, Stella, I beg of you. They'll insist on helping me decorate." He visibly shuddered. "Don't get me wrong, I don't hate Christmas. I just don't love it as much as the rest of my family. I like to keep it simple. They—and by 'they' I mean my very bossy sister—like to turn the entire house into a Christmas wonderland."

She chewed her lower lip as she thought about it. It *would* be nice to have dinner with someone and not by herself. And if Darlene's cookies were anything to go by, the food was probably going to be amazing.

"I'm sorry, Caleb. I just really need to be alone this year."

He frowned. "Why?"

She sucked in a breath. "I just do, okay?"

His eyes searched hers before he nodded. "Okay. I'll do my best to keep my aunt from showing up on your doorstep. I can't promise anything though."

"I won't hold it against you if she does."

"Boomer, come on. Let's go."

The dog barely opened one eyelid. Stella laughed.

"You're such a traitor," Caleb accused.

"He can stay," Stella said. Then she surprised herself by saying, "You can, too. I mean, if you don't already have dinner plans. I have a roast in the Dutch oven.

"That's what smells so good!" He gave his dog the side eye. "And it's probably the reason Boomer doesn't want to leave. He's hoping for his own helping."

"There's enough for both of you."

His head tilted sideways as he searched her face. "Are you sure? You keep saying you want to be alone, so I don't want to intrude."

She offered him a small smile. "I wouldn't ask if I didn't mean it."

"Well, okay then. I would love to stay for dinner."

While she got to work on the roasted Brussel sprouts, which Caleb emphatically told her he would not touch, he poured them both wine. Since he wasn't a fan of Brussel sprouts, she offered to make some steamed broccoli, but he declined that as well.

"The potatoes and carrots are fine," he insisted. "This is a great wine."

She put the sprouts in the oven before joining him at the table. "It's my favorite."

"I figured as much, considering you had a case delivered to my dad's store."

"Is anything a secret around this town?" she teased.

"Nope." When he saw her face, he added, "I'm not kidding. Everyone knows everything about everyone."

The seriousness of his tone had her squirming in her seat. If what he said was true, then that meant people were probably talking about her. The mysterious woman who is hiding out at the lake during the holiday season.

"Hey," Caleb said. "Whatever your reason is for being here it's yours. You don't owe anyone an explanation."

"Thank you," she said softly.

Boomer loped over to them and rested his head in Stella's lap. She automatically began to pet him, the simple act soothing her nerves immediately.

Caleb moved the conversation to the basic get-to-know-one-another topics, but he didn't press when she didn't elaborate. She did tell him her husband had passed away but kept the details to herself, and he let her. She showed him the same courtesy by not being too pushy with her own questions.

When dinner was ready, he helped her bring everything to the table. After they were finished, he even helped her clear the table. He insisted on washing the dishes, so she dried and put them away.

The whole evening was much more pleasant than she had expected. Honestly, she wasn't sure what she expected, especially considering her invitation had been as much a surprise to her as it was to him.

Later that night, as she lie in bed, she found herself content. Not exactly happy, but … better. For the first time in two years, she was finally beginning to feel like herself again.

CHAPTER 9

Thanksgiving was here. While everyone else had woken up at the crack of dawn to get turkeys in the oven, Stella slept in. As she laid in the bed, taking her time to get up for the first time in over twenty years, she reveled in the lack of responsibility for the day. It wasn't just the food and house preparation she was free of; it was also the absence of her responsibility to keep the rest of her family's spirits uplifted. She didn't have to keep a smile plastered on her face. Or keep the conversation focused on the good times. More importantly, she didn't have to fake being okay. It was such a relief to be able to feel however the hell she wanted to that her eyes welled with tears. Last year, she would have wiped them away in an instant—couldn't let the kids see her crying—but this morning she let them fall.

Once she was cried out, she got up and took care of her morning duties before dressing and going downstairs. After she got the coffee going, she took out the small turkey breast and prepared it to go in the slow cooker. As she did so, she smiled to herself, remembering the first Thanksgiving she and Dale shared as a married couple.

Christmas in Evergreen Point

They had just moved to Massachusetts and hadn't made any local friends yet, so it was just the two of them that holiday. Their parents had invited them home, of course, but neither of them wanted to deal with the hassle of traveling. Plus, they were still unpacking and trying to get settled in their new apartment. They decided there was no need for a big turkey, so she'd fixed a turkey breast instead. Then they had put up their new Christmas tree and decorations. Dale had sung off key to Christmas songs as they worked. After they were done and everything was cleaned up, they moved into the kitchen to cook the rest of dinner together.

Dale opened a bottle of white wine and they both sipped as they worked in tandem chopping and mixing and setting timers. By the time they sat down at their small table, they were both a little tipsy from the wine. It had been a great meal. Afterward, they tackled the kitchen clean-up together, then retired to the sofa with another bottle of wine. They turned off all the lights and sat watching the twinkling lights of the tree until retiring to the bedroom, where they made love. The perfect ending to a perfect day.

Sighing now, Stella took her coffee into the living room. The sight of the small table-top artificial tree sitting on the coffee table made her smile. After coffee and breakfast, she would decorate it in honor of that long ago Thanksgiving. She even had wine to sip on as she worked.

The day was slow and pleasant. She took her time decorating her little tree and even added some things to the mantle. She set up her phone to play Christmas music while she cooked in the kitchen. Before she sat down to eat, she checked in with her family over Zoom. They were all at June's house and appeared to be in good spirits, although she could tell that her daughter's smile was forced.

When her own food was ready, Stella sat down to a quiet, small meal, much like that first Thanksgiving with Dale many moons ago.

By the end of the evening, she was on the sofa and watching the flames in the fireplace. She cried a little more. Not sad tears, but tears of acceptance. Cleansing tears.

The sound of a muffled bark, followed by thumping and heavy footsteps on the porch, broke her out of her reverie. She wiped her face as a knock sounded on the front door.

When she opened the door, Caleb's smiling face fell almost immediately.

"Are you okay?" he asked, instantly concerned.

Between them, Boomer gave a low whine. Stella placed a calming hand on his head.

"I'm fine," she said. "Better than fine, actually. How was dinner?"

"The usual." He held up a foil covered pie plate. "Aunt Darlene insisted I bring you a pie. Don't worry, it's not really Thanksgiving-y. Is that even a word? Anyway, it's apple, so think of it as more of a neighborly pie."

Once again, a small laugh escaped her as she took it from him. "I'm not averse to the holiday, you know. Come on in. It's cold."

He came into the house, slipping his shoes off first. "Really? You made it seem like you didn't want anything to do with it."

She took the pie into the kitchen and cut a slice. Caleb declined a piece but accepted a glass of wine. Together, they moved into the living room.

"You have a tree," he pointed out.

She nodded and took a bite of the pie. The second the flavors of tart apple and warm cinnamon hit her taste buds, she closed her eyes and moaned.

"You have a tree," he said again. "Albeit, a tiny one, but it's a Christmas tree."

"This pie is amazing. Yes, it's a Christmas tree. Small enough to pack up and travel with. Why do you seem so surprised?"

He turned and looked at her, his brown eyes swimming in confusion. "I didn't expect it. You've been so anti-holiday that I thought you were avoiding everything to do with both Thanksgiving and Christmas."

Swallowing another delicious bite of pie, she shook her head. "Not at all. As you noticed, I decorated and I also had Thanksgiving dinner tonight." She sent him a small smile. "It's not the holidays I'm trying to avoid. It's everything else that comes with them."

He frowned, his forehead scrunching into a scowl. "I don't understand."

"I needed to be by myself this holiday season."

She could see that he was holding back when he really wanted to pepper her with questions, and she respected him greatly for that. Most people would hound her, demanding an explanation and then further explanation when they didn't understand her reasoning.

"I'm sorry," he said, rising to his feet. "You wanted to be alone, and here I am intruding. I'll go."

"You don't need to go. It's okay. Seriously, Caleb, you are not intruding. Besides, you brought me pie. That gives you an instant pass."

He laughed, deep and throaty. "So that's all it takes? A pie and all is forgiven? I'll need to remember that." He sat back down. "So, you really had a good day here all by yourself?"

"I did."

"But you were crying."

"It was a good kind of cry."

Rolling his eyes, he groaned. "You women always say that, and I never know what it means."

Grinning now, she shook her head. "It's complicated."

"Another frustrating statement." He emptied his glass and went to the kitchen for the bottle. After he poured more into both their glasses, he sank back down beside her. "So, now that I know you're not so anti-holiday, it will be much easier to explain about tomorrow. The town always does it up big the day after Thanksgiving. Everything is decorated. And I mean *everything*. There's even a contest for the best decorated store window."

"That sounds fun."

"It is. The tree lighting in the square is at seven o'clock. There's lots of food, hot chocolate, cider, etcetera, etcetera."

"Sounds like a Hallmark movie."

"Oh, it is *just* like a Hallmark movie." His cheeks turned pink. "Not that I watch those kinds of movies."

She hadn't known the man for long but he was really worked up about this. He reminded her of a kid at, well, Christmas.

"Honestly, I came here to warn you to stay away because I thought you hated everything Christmas."

"You make me sound like the Grinch."

"Well," he said with a shrug of a shoulder. "What else was I supposed to think? Every time the subject came up you would get all ... weird."

Her thoughts drifted back to Dale. Boomer rose and came to rest his head in her lap. His tail thumped a few times on the floor. She stroked his head, giving the occasional rub behind his ears.

"I don't mean to be weird," she said softly. "I'm just ... working through some things."

Nodding slowly, Caleb gazed into the fire. "I get that," he said. "I absolutely get that."

Recognizing the sadness in his voice, Stella watched him carefully. There was a story there, hidden in not only his words, but his eyes, too.

Suddenly, Caleb cleared his throat and stood up. "Well, it's late and I should be getting home. Boomer, come."

Startled, Stella set her glass on the table and got to her feet. "Caleb," she started but he was already at the door and sliding on his boots.

"Thank you for the wine," he said in a rush. "I'll see you around."

"O-okay."

He was already halfway across the yard by the time she reached the door. She called out a thank you for the pie and wished him goodnight before closing the door.

"Now that was weird," she said.

CHAPTER 10

The following morning, Stella went back and forth trying to decide if she should venture into town. She wasn't sure what time the festivities started. Based on Caleb's description last night, she wasn't even sure there was an official start time.

Speaking of Caleb, she had no idea what had happened there. One minute they were relaxing in each other's company and the next, he was running (almost literally) out the door. She tried to recall the exact moment when things went awry, but she'd had so much wine that the details were a little fuzzy. It was also why her head was a little achy today.

Her phone began to ring, drawing her out of her thoughts.

"Hello, June," she answered.

"Hey, Mom. How was your Thanksgiving dinner? Am I even allowed to ask you that?"

Stella stiffened at the hostility in her daughter's voice. "Yes, you may ask me that, and it was nice."

"How could it be nice when you spent the entire day *alone*?"

Biting back a frustrated sigh, Stella explained, "It was exactly what I needed. And for your information, I wasn't entirely alone. Not all day, at least. A neighbor brought over a scrumptious apple pie for dessert and we shared a couple of glasses of wine in front of the fire. It was lovely."

Several heartbeats passed before June spoke again. "I thought you were the only one at the lake. Who is this neighbor?"

"Honey, I told you the caretaker is in the cabin next door. His father is the one who owns the general store in town."

June sucked in a loud, gasping breath. "He? Are you telling me you had a *date* on Thanksgiving?"

With each word June's voice increased in pitch, causing a pinch in Stella's heart.

"It wasn't a date," Stella insisted. "His aunt asked him to bring me a pie because she knew I was alone."

"I can't believe you. It's like you don't even miss him. I have to go."

The accusation was so jolting it took Stella a moment to realize her daughter had ended the call. To think that anyone could entertain the idea that she didn't miss her late husband was unfathomable to her. How could anyone, especially her daughter, think that? And to accuse her of having a date, of all things! A date!

"Of all the unthinkable …" she muttered to herself as she tried to calm herself down.

A date.

Is that really what June thought? Guilt twisted Stella's insides. She needed to fix this. Right now. She dialed June and the call went to voicemail.

"Why that little brat," she hissed as she called Noah.

"Hey, Mom," he answered cheerfully. "How was your quiet Thanksgiving?"

"I think I screwed up. I didn't even think. And now June is mad at me."

"Whoa," Noah said. "Slow down. Why is Junie mad at you? I mean, besides the obvious."

The obvious. Stella huffed out a breath.

"Mom? What happened?"

She explained the phone call with his sister and that Caleb's visit was definitely in no way, shape, or form a date. She didn't even see the man that way. He was barely a friend.

"Oh, boy," Noah said. "Look, Junie is just still upset that you weren't here for Thanksgiving. She missed you terribly."

June always wore her heart on her sleeve, so Stella could only imagine that her behavior yesterday was atrocious.

"Was it bad?" Stella asked. "Was the day horrible because I wasn't there?"

"No. It was … different. And, yeah, Junie was a bit snippy, but when isn't she? Especially lately."

Her heart clenched. "I should have been there. It was selfish of me to think it would be okay if I wasn't."

"Mom, stop. It *was* okay. Junie just still misses dad a lot. We all do. And we missed you, too. *But* we got through it just fine."

A tear of regret slipped down Stella's cheek. "I'm sorry. I just … really needed some time to myself."

"It's okay, Mom. I promise you Junie will get over it."

She sniffled and remained quiet. What was there to say? She'd let her family down.

"I'm glad you did this," Noah said quietly. "I know I was resistant at first, but now … I think I understand."

"You do?"

"Yes. You sound better. Happier or more at peace or something. You obviously needed a break. I'm glad you're getting it. It sucks that it's during the holidays but I'm a big boy. I can handle it."

"And your sister?"

"Believe it or not, I can handle her, too."

Stella laughed. "I know you can. Thank you, Noah."

"You're welcome. Now get back to your bubble baths and truffle eating or whatever it is you're doing there all by yourself."

"Truffles? Really?"

"Maybe it's bonbons. I don't know! Just get back to taking care of yourself."

"I love you."

"And I love you. Now go, and don't worry about Junie. I'll talk to her."

Noah's support eased Stella's nerves and she decided that it would probably be best for her to get out of the cabin for a little bit. If she stayed here by herself, she would dwell on her conversation with June and nothing good would come of that.

So, she bundled up and headed into town. If anything, she could at least get started on her Christmas shopping. She would need to send the presents soon if she wanted them to arrive before the holiday.

When she arrived in town, she was surprised to find the place as crowded as it was. There was even a parking area set up in one of the vacant lots, and it was almost full! Apparently, it wasn't just the locals who lived in town who enjoyed this celebratory event.

Stella parked and headed straight for Darlene's bakery, The Golden Crust. The first thing on her agenda was to thank the woman for her pie and return her plate. The second thing was indulging in one of the woman's famous muffins.

As she approached the bakery, she saw that the most of the store windows along the street had been turned into various Christmas themed scenes, just as Caleb had said. There was everything from snowy forests to colorful Christmas trees and gifts to a cozy fireplace with stockings hanging from the mantle. The window to the bakery was a table covered in a smattering of delectable Christmas goodies, such as pies, cookies, and steaming mugs of hot chocolate.

"Well, hello!" Darlene called out to her from behind the counter.

"Oh, my goodness," Stella said as she looked around the crowded room. There wasn't an empty seat in the place!

She waited in line and then placed her order. A couple of young women were rushing around behind the counter with Darlene. The place was busy, but everyone was smiling and laughing.

"How was your Thanksgiving, dear?" Darlene asked.

"It was nice. Thank you so much for the pie. It was perfect."

"I'm glad you enjoyed it. Poor Caleb was so worried about bringing it to you." She chuckled and shook her head. "That boy. He worries too much."

Stella smiled. Caleb wasn't much of a boy anymore, but she supposed Darlene would always see him that way. Kind of like she did with Noah.

"We had a nice evening," Stella said. "We shared a couple of glasses of wine while I enjoyed your pie. It was a nice visit."

Darlene's eyebrows jumped. "Did you now?"

"He told me about the town celebration today, so I figured I would check it out. Man, he wasn't exaggerating."

"Honey, we're only getting started! Don't go running off or you'll miss out!"

Stella laughed and shook her head. "Don't worry. I'm planning on making a day of it."

"Well, now that's lovely to hear."

"I'll let you get back to work."

Stella took her muffin and coffee to go. She hoped to find a bench somewhere but if not, she could eat and walk.

All around her people were talking and laughing. She still couldn't believe the transformation the town had seemingly taken overnight. Of course, it could have started days ago. She hadn't been in town for a few days.

Taking everything in, Stella finished her breakfast as she explored. There were vendors set up for what she assumed was the tree lighting later on this evening. They weren't selling food yet, but she noted signs for everything from hot pretzels to hot chocolate and cider. There was even a cart selling roasted chestnuts!

"Wow," Stella said out loud.

"It's pretty amazing, isn't it?" a woman said.

Turning, Stella almost gasped. It was like looking at a female version of Caleb. "You must be Caleb's sister."

Startled, the woman said, "Uh, yeah. I'm Celia."

"Oh, I'm sorry. My name is Stella. I'm renting the cabin at the lake."

"Oh! Of course! Nice to meet you. Are you enjoying your visit?"

"I am."

Celia nodded, her eyes focusing over Stella's shoulder. "That's great to hear. I'm sorry, but you'll have to excuse me. I need to go find my kids before they terrorize the whole town. Maybe we'll catch up later?"

"Okay."

Stella watched as the woman ran across the street and nabbed two boys just as they were about to send a display table toppling over. Oh, boy. The woman definitely had her hands full.

Going over her gift list in her head, Stella headed for the nearest store.

CHAPTER 11

Later that afternoon and four trips back to her car, Stella sank onto a bench in front of the general store. She'd completed almost all of her shopping. Checking the time on her phone, she saw that it was nearing five o'clock. She was hungry and the savory and sugary smells wafting through the air weren't helping.

The food vendors had opened an hour ago and the lines had been steady. Stella still couldn't believe how many people were here. It was crazy.

Something cold and wet brushed against her hand, making her yelp in surprise. Boomer responded with a loving lick, making her laugh.

"Hey, buddy," she said as she leaned over and kissed his head.

"Stella, hi."

She looked up and found Caleb walking towards her. "Hey! Wow, you weren't kidding about this!"

"I told you." His smile was cautious and fleeting. "Sorry about Boomer. He just gets so excited when he sees you."

"That's okay. We're buds, aren't we, Boomer?"

The dog wagged happily.

"Sorry," Caleb apologized again, making her frown. "I have to go help my dad. I hope you enjoy the tree lighting. Boomer, come!"

Confused, Stella watched the man and dog disappear into the store. What in the world was that about? Why was Caleb suddenly acting so strange around her? She had hoped he would have gotten past whatever had thrown him last night, but apparently that wasn't the case.

Tossing those thoughts aside, she abandoned her resting spot and headed for the group of food vendors. She decided on a slice of pizza. There were several picnic benches grouped together in a little eating area. She was lucky enough to find a spot to sit and enjoy her slice while watching the excitement around her.

The tree in the square was fully decorated and beginning to draw a crowd around it, even though there was still over an hour and a half to go before the official lighting.

"Isn't it a little early to be gathering around the tree?" she asked someone at a neighboring table.

"Oh, not at all. The caroling starts at six. Then there's the raffle winner announcements and the address by the mayor."

"Oh, okay. I had no idea."

The man smiled. "First time?"

"Yes. I've been renting a cabin at the lake for a few weeks."

"In this weather?" the man cried, making her laugh. "Well, welcome to Evergreen. I hope you're enjoying your visit."

"I am."

63

It was puzzling how everyone had the same reaction when they found out she was renting the cabin. Even more so now that she saw this Christmas festival taking place. Honestly, she was surprised the rest of the lake homes were empty. It seemed like a missed opportunity, not only for guests to enjoy the festivities, but also for more revenue for town businesses.

Not that they really needed it, she thought as she looked around at the crowd milling about. The town definitely wasn't hurting for money today.

When it was close to time for the mayor to speak, Stella wandered over to get in line for a hot chocolate. Since most people were gathered around the tree, the line was the shortest it had been all day. Once she took her first sip, she understood why.

"Oh, my," she whispered.

"Best cup of hot chocolate you've ever had?" a woman beside her asked.

"Yes, it is. Wow."

The mayor called for everyone's attention. She welcomed everyone and introduced the head of the planning committee who would announce the winners of the raffle and window decorating contest.

Caleb appeared beside her, gently nudging her arm. "Having fun?"

"I really am. You were right; this is quite the celebration."

He smiled. "I see you got some of Mary's magnificent hot chocolate. I don't know what she puts in that stuff, but it's delicious."

Chuckling, Stella said, "You mean she hasn't shared her secret recipe? Shocking."

He rolled his eyes playfully and then went on alert. "Oh, here we go. I hope Dad wins this year. He and Aunt Darlene were up half the night painting the store window."

Her eyes rounded. "They painted that in one night? Wow."

Unfortunately, Howie didn't come in first place. He did come in second though. The hardware store won the top prize with its 'Christmas by the Fire' scene.

"Ah, well," Caleb said.

"Hey, second place is nothing to scoff at," Stella said. "The competition was fierce."

"It's almost time. Let's move a little closer."

They inched closer, joining the outer edge of the crowd just in time for the caroling to begin. Stella couldn't remember the last time she'd been caroling. She had to have been a kid. It was more fun than she remembered. Probably because it was such a large group and everyone was in great spirits.

After the caroling, the mayor took the stand again. The countdown began and then the tree lit up. Everyone cheered and then oohed and awed.

"It's amazing," Stella murmured as she looked at the giant tree covered in lights, garland, and ornaments galore.

Her throat tightened. Dale would have loved this. The tree, the hot chocolate, all of it.

"Hey, are you okay?" Caleb asked.

She nodded. "This is the perfect end to a wonderful day."

"End? The night's not over."

She turned to him in surprise. "There's more?"

Grinning, he shook his head. "The party will keep going until around nine, but people will start leaving soon. It's been a long day."

"Yes, it has. Long but lovely."

"I'm glad you enjoyed it." He took her by the hand and gave a gentle tug. "You need to come say hi to Dad or he'll be crushed. He's been asking about you all day."

They made their way to the store, where the second-place ribbon hung proudly in the window. When they entered, Howie looked up from the shelf he was stocking and smiled.

"Hello, Stella! Did you enjoy the tree lighting?" he asked.

"Yes, I did! Congratulations on second place, by the way."

"Thank you." He gestured to a chair by the counter. "Take a seat. I bet your feet are tired."

"They are that." She sank onto the stool and sighed. When her sigh turned into a yawn, she covered it with her hand. "Oh, my. Excuse me."

"I'm right there with you," Howie said. "It's been a heck of a long day."

Finished with his stocking, he passed the now empty box to Caleb, who took it out the back to the trash, and then came to sit next to Stella.

"I hope my son hasn't been harassing you too much. I know my sister was pushing him about dinner yesterday. I'm sorry for that."

"It's okay, and no, Caleb has definitely not been harassing me. I barely see him. He pretty much stays in his cabin most days."

Howie nodded. "That sounds like Caleb. I'm glad he's not interfering with your vacation. I heard you met my daughter earlier today."

"I did. Um, Howie, I hope this isn't too forward of me, but are you not married?"

The older man shifted on his stool. "In my heart, yes. My wife passed about five years ago."

She reached out and squeezed his hand. "I'm so sorry. I lost my husband a couple of years ago."

He nodded. "I figured that was the case. You have that lingering sadness in your eyes. I still see it in the mirror sometimes myself. I'm sorry for your loss, Stella."

"Thank you. I, ah, really haven't told anyone around here."

"No worries. One thing I'm not is a gossip."

The sting in her eyes caught her off guard. "Thank you," she said softly. "I appreciate that."

Caleb reappeared with Boomer on his heels. The dog rushed to Stella and she couldn't help but smile as she pet him. Then she got to her feet and said goodnight before heading to her car. By the time she got back to the cabin, she was half asleep on her feet, so she left all of her purchases in the car for the night. She didn't think anyone would bother them way out here.

She fell asleep almost before her head hit the pillow.

CHAPTER 12

The next day, Stella spent the morning wrapping the gifts she'd purchased. By the afternoon, the temperature had warmed up enough for her daily nature walk. She went next door in search of her walking partner. Caleb answered the door looking distracted. Boomer, of course, was excited to see her.

"Everything okay?" Stella asked.

"Hmm?" Caleb looked bewildered. "Oh, yes. Everything is fine. Going for your walk?"

"Yes, now that it's warmed up a bit."

"Good. Thanks for letting Boomer join you."

"No, thank *you*."

There was definitely something going on with him. She couldn't help but wonder if it had to do with his abrupt exit the other night. She still hadn't figured out what that had been about. She hadn't thought much about it since yesterday he was back to his usual happy self. Now he was closed off again. She wasn't sure what to make of it.

"I'll bring him back in a bit," she said.

"Okay." Already turning away, he closed the door.

She looked down at Boomer and said, "What in the world is going on with him?"

Tongue hanging out of the side of his mouth, Boomer wagged his tail.

"All right. Let's go, shall we?"

They followed their usual trail around the lake. Stella wondered what she was going to do when she left. She'd grown accustomed to these daily jaunts and would hate to give them up. Maybe she didn't have to. She would just have to figure out a way to indulge in a walk at home every day. Perhaps there was a walking trail nearby. She would have to check.

When they returned, Stella took Boomer to her cabin and gave him a bowl of water and a couple of dog treats she'd bought yesterday while in town. He gobbled them up with gusto.

"Okay, Boomer," she said. "I think it's time to take you back. Hopefully, Caleb will be in a better mood."

He wasn't. He was still thoroughly distracted, so she left him to whatever it was that had his attention. She returned to cabin and found her phone ringing.

She smiled when she saw Noah's name. "Hello, Noah!"

"Hey, Mom. Are you okay? You sound out of breath."

"I'm great. I just got back from my daily walk and had to rush inside to get to the phone."

"Daily walk? Isn't it cold?"

"Well, yes, but when you're walking it's not so bad."

"Oh. I suppose. Anyway, Junie asked me to call and check on you because you didn't answer her call. I think she was worried you're avoiding her because you're mad at her."

"I'm not mad at all. I just didn't take my phone with me. I'll call her as soon as I get off the phone with you."

"Okay. Um, Mom, do you think it's a good idea to go walking alone without your phone?"

His concern warmed her heart, and she felt slightly guilty about making him worry.

"Honey, the reception isn't very good around the lake. Besides, I'm not alone. Boomer, the neighbor's dog, usually goes with me. If something happens, he would run home and get Caleb."

Her explanation was met with an awkward silence.

"Noah, are you still there?" she asked.

"I'm here. I think I agree with Junie. I'm not sure I'm comfortable with you being out there by yourself with some strange man. What if he's dangerous?"

Stella couldn't hold back her laughter. "Honey, I assure you I am perfectly safe here. Caleb is a nice man. His family owns several businesses in town."

"You've met his family?"

"Well, yes. His father owns the general store, his aunt owns the bakery, and his sister owns the rental company through which I rented the cabin. And trust me when I say the whole town is friendly. It's quite lovely actually. You should see it."

The sound of shuffling papers filled the background as Noah said, "Maybe I will. Next weekend. How about I come for a visit?"

This wasn't part of the deal, but Stella found herself delighted with the idea. Even if her son's true intention was to check up on her, she would love to see him.

"That would be lovely," she said. "But aren't you busy with work?"

"That's why I'll come for the weekend. Unless you don't want me to come."

"Of course I would love to see you!"

"Okay, then it's settled. I will be there Friday evening."

"Okay, see you then."

After they hung up, she took a few minutes to herself before she dialed her daughter but got her voicemail. She didn't leave a message, opting instead to send a text, in which she apologized for missing her call and explained she was out for a walk. June replied that she was in a meeting and would catch up with her later.

Stella grabbed her tablet and spent the rest of the afternoon reading. Then she fixed herself a leftover turkey sandwich for dinner. It was a simple meal, but she didn't want to waste the leftovers. She took her sandwich into the living room to eat while she turned on a Christmas movie. The celebration yesterday had done its job and put her in the holiday mood.

CHAPTER 13

The next week flew by in a flurry of preparations for Noah's upcoming visit. Stella went back into town and stocked up on the fixings for his favorite meal, her homemade lasagna. She also bought the ingredients for holiday cookies. Baking those took almost an entire day and she loved every minute of it. She made sure there was plenty to send home with Noah so that he could share with June's family.

Thursday afternoon she was sitting on the sofa and looking at her small table-top tree. Should she get a bigger one? This little one was perfect for just her, but now that Noah was coming to visit, she felt obligated to have a more traditional tree. But didn't that go against everything this trip was originally about? The whole reason for coming here was to get way from all the stress of the traditional holiday. To avoid all of the normal expectations. Now, here she was considering buying a tree and decorations *and* she'd even baked a bunch of Christmas cookies!

She scoffed at herself. Baking was never stressful for her. In fact, it was just the opposite. She enjoyed baking, especially when it was for her family. She felt a small twinge in her chest. Dale had loved her Christmas cookies the most.

Come to think of it, he would have laughed at her little tree. She could hear him now. *That is* not *a tree, Stella*. Smiling, she told herself it was enough for her, but Noah deserved a regular tree.

Stella put her boots on and grabbed her coat. If she was going to get a tree, then she was going to need some help. There was no way she could carry it on her own, so she headed for Caleb's.

Her excitement waned when he answered the door. His hair was a mess and his clothes were slightly wrinkled. There were shadows under his eyes as well.

"Oh, my. Are you sick?" she asked.

Blinking in confusion, he said, "No, I'm fine. Why would you ask me that?"

"It's just that you look ..." She gestured to his clothes.

Looking down, he assessed his appearance. "Oh. I've just been busy working."

"All night?"

"Yes, actually. Well, most of it." He glanced over his shoulder before turning back to her. "Are you going for your walk?"

"Um, no, I was going to ask a favor of you, but now that I see that you're busy, never mind."

"Hmm." He nodded. "Okay. See you later then."

And then the door was shut in her face. Taken aback, Stella just stared at it.

"Well, okay then," she muttered, turning to leave.

She got into her car and drove into town by herself. Maybe she would get lucky and the Christmas tree lot would deliver the tree. After all, everyone was so friendly and helpful here.

But first, she needed more decorations, so she went into the boutique she remembered that carried some of the prettiest ornaments she'd ever seen. While she was checking out, she inquired about the tree.

"Oh, I'm sure it won't be a problem getting it to your place," Cindy, the manager, said. "Hang on just a second."

The woman picked up her phone and tapped a few buttons. "Hey, Mitch. Stella is here asking after a tree but she needs it delivered to the Anderson's place. Can you make that happen?" Listening, she nodded. "Great! I'll send her your way." She set the phone down and smiled. "You're good to go. Mitch said it won't be a problem at all."

"Thank you. I didn't mean for you to go to any trouble."

"Oh, honey, don't even worry about it. It's no trouble at all helping out a friend."

Touched at being considered a friend, Stella nodded. "Thank you."

She put her bags in the back seat of her car and then drove to the edge of town where the tree was located.

"You must be Stella," a big man bundled up like a lumberjack greeted her.

"I am. You're Mitch?"

He nodded. "Cindy said you're looking for a tree. I have a great one in mind. Should look great in the Anderson's cabin."

"Okay."

She followed him to the middle of the lot, where he showed her a tree that while, a little bigger than she had planned for, it seemed perfect for the cabin. She could already envision it in the corner of the living room.

"Wow," she whispered. "It's lovely. I think you're right, Mitch. It's perfect."

"You should still have a look around and make sure."

She shook her head. "I don't think I'll find a better one. This one is big, symmetrical, and very full. How in the world has it not sold already?"

"Because it was waiting for you." Mitch's eyes twinkled in delight. "I'll have Dennis deliver it your place in about an hour or so."

"Thank you so much."

Stella paid him and then was on her way back to the cabin in no time. She carried her bags inside and then made quick work of making room for the tree. By the time she was done, a truck pulled into the driveway. She went outside to meet the delivery guy, who carried the tree inside and helped her get it situated in the stand. She thanked him and offered him a tip but he declined.

Alone now with her tree, Stella fixed some hot tea and stoked the fire. Then she sat down and looked at the big fir tree. It would take some time for the branches to settle so she would wait on decorating it. Breathing deeply, she inhaled the familiar scent and closed her eyes as Dale's voice came back to her.

The best thing about a live tree is the smell. There's nothing like it.

Having grown up with only ever having an artificial tree, she'd always thought a Christmas tree was a Christmas tree. It was the lights and decorations that made it.

She was wrong.

Dale was right.

Sighing, Stella opened her eyes. What a fool she'd been to think that a small, artificial tree would be good enough.

Later that evening, she turned on some Christmas music and got to work decorating. After she unpacked her shopping bags, she realized she might have gone a little overboard. Tree decorations weren't the only decorations she'd bought. There was a beautiful centerpiece made of striped candles and holly branches, an adorable reindeer salt and pepper shaker set, and several other knick-knack type things.

"How in the world am I going to get all of this home?" she wondered aloud.

Dale's voice filled her mind once again. *You can never have too much Christmas.*

Stella snorted. You absolutely could have too much Christmas *stuff*. Especially when you already owned numerous tubs of decorations already at home as Stella did.

"Oh, well," she said with a sigh. She would worry about that later.

She arranged the centerpiece on the table, along with the salt and pepper set. Then she went into the kitchen and made herself a Hot Toddy to sip on while she tackled the tree.

CHAPTER 14

An hour and two Hot Toddies later, Stella jumped when a knock sounded at her door. Even though it was late, she called out that the door was open.

Boomer ran inside, barking joyously in greeting. Caleb followed. When he saw the tree, he stopped short.

"Hi!" Stella said brightly, leaning over to pet Boomer. "To what do I owe this surprise visit?"

Caleb looked at her with wide eyes. "Someone has been bitten by the Christmas bug. What did I miss?"

"Noah is coming to visit this weekend."

"And Noah is?"

"Oh! My son. I really think he's coming to check up on you but he's going to be here for the weekend so I figured I should decorate for him."

"Whoa, slow down." Head tilted, Caleb frowned. "Are you drunk?"

She laughed. "I've had two Hot Toddies. Would you like one?"

"Uh, I'll take some whisky, hold the tea."

"Coming right up!" She rushed across the room into the kitchen.

"Maybe I should just pour my own drink," Caleb suggested.

"What? Don't be silly. I need another one myself."

"Stella," Caleb rested a hand on her arm. "Are you sure that's a good idea? It seems like you've had plenty. You don't want to be hungover when your son arrives tomorrow, do you?"

"Oh, please. I won't be hungover."

He muttered something under his breath that sounded suspiciously like 'famous last words', and she whirled around.

"What is your problem lately?" she snapped. "You've been acting strangely all week. And now you're here trying to ruin what has been a festive evening with your negativity. What's the deal? Did I do something to offend you?"

He gently took his drink from her and sipped it. "You're right. I'm sorry. I know I haven't been acting friendly lately. That's why I'm here. To apologize."

She didn't respond, choosing to stare at him expectantly.

He sighed. "Stella, I'm sorry. I've been a little preoccupied with work. I have a deadline to meet, and I've fallen behind. I shouldn't take it out on you though."

"Deadline?" She scrunched her forehead. "Are you a writer or something?"

"I am."

That explained why he would hole himself up inside his house for days on end.

"So earlier when I came over—"

"I was working and it wasn't going well. It was only after I finished, I realized how poorly I'd treated you." He looked at the tree in the corner. "I'm assuming you were going to ask me to help you get the tree here."

She nodded.

"How did you manage that by yourself, by the way? It's huge."

"Mitch had Dennis deliver it."

Caleb raised his eyebrows in surprise. "Really? Mitch and Dennis, huh? You're starting to sound like a local."

"Yes, well, *some* people around here are welcoming." She carried her drink past him and sat on the sofa. "Isn't that right, Boomer?"

The dog set his head in her lap. Caleb joined them, sinking down beside Stella.

"So, you said your son is coming to check me out?" He paused and cleared his throat. "Uh, what does that mean exactly?"

She waved a hand in the air. "He wants to make sure you're not a serial killer or something."

He burst into laughter. She couldn't hold back and found herself joining in.

"And why, may I ask, would he think that?" Caleb asked. "I know I've been a little moody, but a serial killer?"

She told him about her conversation with June, which led to Noah feeling the need to come and check up on her. As he listened, Caleb nodded.

"I get it," he said when her explanation was done. "They're worried about you."

She nodded. "I understand that. I do. It's just … June was so angry. She has been about this whole trip."

"Of course she is. You're her mother. It's Christmas. Add to that the fact that she misses her father."

Tears welled in Stella's eyes and she shook them away. "I miss him, too. That's why I needed this trip. Dale loved the holidays. Without him, it's ..." She took a second to swallow back the tears that still threatened to spill over. "It's not the same. It never will be again. I needed to get away from all of *that*."

"You came here to heal," Caleb said softly. "By yourself."

"Yes." She choked out a sob and he gathered her in his arms.

"Stella, there's nothing wrong with taking some time for yourself. Sure, your kids are upset now, but when they look back on this in the future, they'll see that."

"They made me feel so horrible. Like I was abandoning them." She wiped her cheeks. "For the past two years, I've been there for them. To make things easier for *them*. To help *them* grieve."

"Meanwhile, you didn't allow *yourself* time to grieve. At least not properly." He smoothed her hair back over her shoulder. "You deserve time to grieve, too. Not only that, but you deserve to do it *your* way."

Sending him a grateful smile, she said, "Thank you."

Boomer whined and nudged her knee. She automatically reached out to him. With each pass of her hand over his soft head, she felt better. After a few minutes, she drew in a big breath.

"I'm so sorry," she said. "I guess I might have had a little too much to drink after all."

Chuckling, Caleb said, "Maybe, but you don't need to apologize."

She looked into his eyes and felt a stirring deep inside her. It was so unexpected that it stole the breath from her lungs. Swallowing hard, she lunged to her feet.

"I-I think I should call it a night," she said quickly. "You should go. Thank you for checking on me, but you should go now."

"Okay." Caleb slowly rose. "Are you sure you're all right?"

"I'm fine."

He nodded. "Goodnight then."

She walked him to the door, leaning against it once it had closed behind him. She took several deep breaths and then turned off the music and lights and went upstairs to bed.

CHAPTER 15

The next day was a blur of cleaning and preparation in anticipation of Noah's arrival. Once his room was ready and the downstairs was cleaned and straightened, she set to work boiling the noodles and setting out the rest of the ingredients for the lasagna.

All day she tried to convince herself that she wasn't nervous about Noah's visit. There was no need to be worried. She was sure that Noah would like the town. Once he saw how charming it was and how friendly the people were, any reservations he had about her staying here would be put to rest. Especially once he met Caleb.

Her stomach fluttered at the thought of her neighbor. She was so embarrassed by her behavior last night. Knowing Caleb, he probably wouldn't even comment about her break down.

Oh, God. What if he did? Even worse, what if he brought it up *in front of Noah*? Surely her son would insist on her returning home then. So would June when she found out.

She pressed a hand to her stomach. That was silly. Caleb wouldn't do that to her. Would he? She'd told him how worried her children already were about her.

The timer beeped, drawing her back to the task at hand. She drained the noodles and took them over to the counter so she could begin assembling the dish. She hummed along to the Christmas music she had playing on her phone.

When the lasagna was ready, she popped it in the oven. Then she gave the cabin a final once-over. Even though it was a rental, she thought she'd done a great job at making it festive and homey.

She went upstairs to shower and change. By the time she returned downstairs, the comforting scents of garlic and basil had filled the air, enveloping her in a mouth-watering hug. Her stomach growled in response, reminding her that she'd skipped lunch.

Oh, well. If she ate something now, she'd ruin her dinner.

The sound of barking drew her to the sliding back door. She spotted Boomer and Caleb playing fetch on the lakeshore. Smiling, she stepped out onto the back porch and called out to them.

"Hey!" Caleb said with a wave.

Boomer, of course, ran straight towards her. Laughing, she leaned over to kiss the top of his head. She took the stick from him and tossed it through the air. While he raced after it, Caleb walked up to her porch.

"Is Noah here yet?" he asked.

"No. He should be here any minute though."

Caleb nodded. "I thought I'd try to wear Boomer out some before dinner, so he won't be too much."

"Are you kidding? He's the most well-behaved dog I've ever seen."

"Okay, so maybe I'm the one who needed to get out of the house to take my mind off of some things."

She frowned. "Everything okay?"

"Yeah." He shook his head and gave her a sheepish smile. "Would it be weird if I told you that I'm nervous about meeting your son?"

"What? Why?"

Tucking his hands in his front pockets, he shrugged. "I mean, the only reason he's coming is to check me out. It's a lot of unexpected pressure."

For some reason, his confession made her stomach do a little shimmy. Stupid nerves.

"I'm sure that's not the only reason he's coming," she said, hoping to ease his anxiety. "Would it make you feel any better if I told you I'm nervous, too?"

"You are?" He ran his fingers and thumb along his jawline. "Huh. I guess that does make me feel better."

Boomer returned with his stick and Stella threw it again. Then she hugged herself against the cold. It probably would have been a good idea to grab her coat before coming out here.

"You're freezing," Caleb said. "You should go back inside. I'm going to go feed Boomer and clean up. I'll see you in a bit."

"Okay."

She went back inside and straight to the fireplace to warm up. A few minutes later, she heard a car honk outside and went to the front door.

"Hello!" she called as Noah got out of the car. She ran down the steps and caught him in a giant hug.

"Hey, Mom." He looked at the cabin. "It's bigger than I expected."

"Yes, well, that's a good thing. It means I have plenty of room for you to visit."

He laughed. "That is true."

"Come on. Grab your stuff and let's get inside where it's warm."

She led him into the house and spun around. "Ta da! Don't you just love it?"

Noah's jaw dropped as he looked around the cabin. He clamped his mouth shut when he saw the huge tree in the corner.

Slowly lowering her arms to her sides, her proud smile faded and Stella asked, "Don't you like it?"

"Uh, yeah. I'm just confused. I thought you came here to get away from all of the Christmas hoopla."

"Well, yes, but when I found out you were coming, I decided to decorate a little more."

His face softened. "So, this is all for me? Aw, Mom, you didn't have to do this if it's not what you wanted. That wasn't my intention coming here. Now I feel bad."

She gave his arm a squeeze. "Don't you dare feel bad! I actually enjoyed decorating, and I think it makes the place feel more like home." She looked around proudly. "Don't you think so?"

Noah nodded.

"Now, your room is upstairs on the left. Go put your things away and then come back down. Dinner should be ready soon."

Watching Noah disappear up the stairs, she bit her lip. Had she screwed up again? She thought he would appreciate the effort she'd put in for his visit. Instead, he seemed irritated. She didn't understand. Fighting tears, she went into the kitchen to butter and garlic the bread.

Noah came back downstairs. "Anything I can do to help?"

"I've got it under control. You just relax. All that's left is the salad."

As she got to work on the salad, they chatted about Noah's drive and how things were going back at home. She'd just set the big bowl of salad on the table when Boomer barked outside, announcing his and Caleb's arrival.

Stella called out that the door was unlocked, and seconds later Boomer raced into the cabin. He ran straight to the kitchen, sat, and looked at Stella. She laughed and got him a treat from the cabinet while she introduced Noah and Caleb.

The two men shook hands before Caleb turned to her. "I brought wine."

Eyeing the label, she grinned. "Perfect. I'll get the corkscrew. Have a seat."

"Nah, you sit. I'll pour the wine." He looked at Noah. "Would you like a glass or would you prefer something else?"

"Wine is fine. Thanks."

Stella couldn't help but notice the way her son watched Caleb as he confidently moved around the kitchen. His judgement was evident in the crease of his brow and the way his eyes tracked the other man. The set of his jaw suggested that he was determined to not like the man, which was unusual for Noah.

Stella sat down at the table while Caleb poured their drinks. When she caught Noah's eye, she sent him a smile.

"So," Noah said when Caleb joined them. "You're the caretaker here?"

"Unofficially," Caleb answered. He went into the same explanation he'd given Stella. "Also, my dad owns the general store and my aunt owns the bakery."

"And your mother?"

"She passed away five years ago."

"I'm sorry."

Caleb nodded. "I'm sorry about your father."

The tension in the room pulsed at the mention of Dale. Stella tried to steer the conversation to happier topics by bringing up the town's earlier Christmas celebration.

"We do it all again on Christmas Eve," Caleb said. "Well, a smaller version because it's a busy day for everyone."

"Oh! No one told me that," Stella said as she got up to swap the lasagna for the bread in the oven. "Just about ten more minutes or so and we should be good to go."

While the two men continued to chat, she brought everything to the table, ending with the toasted garlic bread.

CHAPTER 16

Dinner was pleasant, as the conversation remained mostly trivial. After they were finished, the three of them worked together to clear the table and clean up the dishes.

When the kitchen was clean, Noah excused himself to the restroom. Caleb took this brief respite to ask Stella how she was holding up.

"I'm okay," she said. "He seems so guarded and I really don't understand why."

"You're his mother and he's protective."

She nodded uncertainly as Noah came into the living room.

"You know," he said, looking at Caleb. "I can't help but feel like I know you from somewhere. You seem very familiar."

Smiling coyly, Caleb said, "Well, you've probably seen my picture before. Do you read?"

Noah's eyes bulged and he gasped. "No way! You're C.J. Abrahams?"

"Yes, I am."

Looking back and forth between the two men, Stella said, "I'm lost." Then the realization hit her, making her gasp in surprise just as her son had done. "Wait a minute! Are you telling me you are a famous author? *That* C.J. Abrahams?"

Although she hadn't read any of his work, she'd heard other people talk about his books, including June.

Looking sheepish, Caleb nodded. "The one and only."

She couldn't believe she hadn't put it together before now.

"So, do you live in the cabin full time?" Noah asked.

"When I'm not traveling for work. That's why I'm the unofficial caretaker around here."

"That makes sense," Noah said before turning to Stella. "You really had no idea?"

She shook her head.

"The details of my occupation never really came up," Caleb explained.

"When you said you were a writer, I just assumed you worked for the local paper or an online blog or something," Stella said. "I can't believe you didn't tell me."

"It's not something I like to draw attention to," Caleb replied.

"Why not?" Noah asked. "You're an amazing writer! You should be proud."

Cheeks reddening, Caleb said, "Most of us writers like to keep a low profile, if we can. You know, the whole introversion thing."

"I can't believe my mom is friends with C.J. Abrahams! This is so cool!"

Stella chuckled while poor Caleb looked into the fire. His discomfort was starting to roll off of him in waves, so she turned the tables and asked Noah how his job was going. Even though the young man clearly didn't want to discuss his boring office job, he caught the hint and went along with the change in topic.

Finally, Noah's day got the best of him and he excused himself to retire upstairs. Stella saw Caleb and Boomer to the door.

"Thank you for coming to dinner," she said. "I'm so sorry he put you on the spot like that."

"It's okay. Thank you for inviting me. It was delicious. The best lasagna I've ever eaten."

"Oh, don't be silly."

"I'm serious. I usually only eat the frozen stuff."

"Well, I'm glad you enjoyed it. I guess I'll see you tomorrow?"

"Mm. Maybe. I still have that deadline to meet, so I might be MIA."

"Okay. Goodnight, Caleb."

"Goodnight, Stella."

After he left, she fixed herself a cup of tea and sat back down in front of the fire to wind down a little more. It had been a busy and exciting day, albeit stressful as well.

"Hey, Mom," Noah said as came down the stairs.

"I thought you went to bed."

"Not yet." He yawned. "But I'm not going to last too much longer. I thought you might like to read one of Caleb's books now that you know who he is."

"You're too young to be so tired." She chuckled as she took the paperback from him. "Thanks."

"Well, it's been a long week."

Frowning, she said, "I hope this trip didn't cause issues with your work schedule."

"No, not at all."

"Good. So, I take it you no longer think Caleb is a serial killer?"

"A serial killer, no, but just because he's a well-known author doesn't mean he couldn't be taking advantage of you." She began to protest but he cut her off. "However, after meeting him, I think he's a good guy. I still can't believe I've read almost every book he's written. It's kind of surreal."

"What kind of books does he write?"

"Mysteries. You really didn't recognize him?"

She shook her head. "I've never read his books, so how could I? It explains his moodiness though."

They shared a laugh this time.

"So, is your sister still upset with me?"

He sighed. "She's … frustrated. Your not being home for Thanksgiving was hard, and Christmas isn't going to be any easier."

"I know. I'm sorry."

He gazed around the room, finally settling on the giant Christmas tree. "I have to admit that I'm still a little confused myself. You said you didn't want to deal with all of the 'hoopla' around the holiday, yet here you are decorating a house that isn't even yours and attending the local holiday festivities."

She bit the inside of her cheek as she tried to find the right words to express her feelings. Honestly, she was getting tired of trying to explain herself. It was exhausting.

"It almost feels as if it's us you needed to get away from," Noah said. "I think that's why Junie is so upset."

Swallowing, Stella nodded. "I can see that. It's not that I don't want to be with you two, it's just that I needed some time to grieve for myself, *by myself*, without the reminders of your father or the pressures of his absence staring me in the face every time I turned around. I don't know how else to explain it. I thought I didn't want all of the 'hoopla', but now I'm starting to see that that isn't true."

His eyes, so much like his father's, searched her face. "I guess that kind of makes sense. Last year you were so great about making sure the holidays were great for us."

"I needed time to grieve in my own way."

"I'm sorry. It wasn't fair of us to rob you of that."

"Oh, you didn't!" She gripped his hand. "I chose to put my grief on hold for you. This year would have been the same if I'd stayed. I'm your mother and it's always been my job to put your needs before my own." She released his hand and gestured around the room. "Here, I can't do that."

Noah nodded. "I get that. Maybe you should try telling June all of this."

"I have. She isn't ready to listen."

The side of his mouth lifted in a smirk. "I think you're right about that." The smirk disappeared. "She's really been struggling, mostly because she is so worried about you."

"What? Why?"

He shrugged. "She said something about losing you, too."

Pain pierced Stella's heart. What in the world did that mean? She wasn't planning on going anywhere. Yet, she had. She'd disappeared during the biggest family time of the year. Was June worried that she wasn't going to come back?

"Okay, I really need to get some sleep," Noah said, standing up and stretching. "'Night, Mom."

"Goodnight, Noah."

She kissed his cheek and then followed him up the stairs. As she got ready for bed, she thought about what she could possibly do, short of packing up and returning home, to try to patch things up with her daughter.

CHAPTER 17

The next day, Stella cooked a big breakfast for Noah before taking him into town. She introduced him to everyone as they shopped and then enjoyed a quick lunch at the local pub. Afterward, they returned to the cabin and went on a walk together.

Of course, Boomer joined them, leading the way.

"You do this every day?" Noah asked when they stopped for a short break to play fetch with Boomer.

"I try to."

Rubbing his gloved hands together, Noah said, "Even in this weather? Are you crazy?"

She laughed softly. "You get used to it, and it's not so bad as long as you keep moving."

"And this dog always comes with you?"

"Yes, he does. If I leave without him, he throws a fit until Caleb opens the door so he can catch up with me."

Noah watched as Boomer returned with the stick in his mouth. When the dog dropped it and went into downward dog with his rump in the air Noah laughed.

"He's a good boy," Stella said as she tossed the stick. "I've enjoyed his companionship so much that

I'm considering getting my own dog when I come home."

"Seriously?"

"Yeah. The house is so empty now. It's lonely."

"Then maybe you should get a dog." He looked at her with sad eyes. "I'm sorry I never thought about how hard it must be for you to face that emptiness every day."

"Oh, honey, that's not your responsibility."

"But still."

Boomer jogged back to her and wiggled around her legs.

"It's time to go back, isn't it, boy?" Stella said and was rewarded with a joyful bark.

On their walk back, Noah told her that he loved the small town and could see why she was happy here. It warmed her heart that he'd let go of his reservations.

"So, you're not going to tie me up, toss me in the back of your car, and take me home?" she teased.

"That was never the plan." He kicked at a rock. "I just needed to see with my own eyes that you were okay."

"I am. In fact, I'm much better than when I first arrived."

"I see that. You're ... happy. More than that. Content."

She was pretty sure the two words meant the same thing, but somehow what he was saying made sense. She felt at peace here. Hopefully, that wouldn't change when she went home. The possibility made her sad. What if she couldn't be happy at home without Dale?

"Dammit, I made you sad," Noah said. "I'm sorry."

"Will you stop apologizing to me! And no, *you* didn't make me sad. I was just thinking about your dad. Missing him."

Noah sighed. "Yeah."

They returned Boomer to Caleb and once they were inside the cabin, they warmed up in front of fire. Noah checked his phone and then excused himself to make a call upstairs.

Stella was pretty sure he was calling his sister to give her a status update, so she left him to it. She'd already decided that once Noah left, she would call June herself. It was past time that they finally hashed things out between them. That is, if June would allow it. She could only hope that Noah's visit would help her daughter see things from her perspective.

Stella hated that they were at odds, but she had tried to appease her daughter the best she could. The first step to getting past the grief of losing Dale was Stella dealing with hers. Only then could June stop worrying about her and work on dealing with her own grief.

Maybe she should just invite June here so she could see for herself how good this trip was for Stella.

A soft gasp slipped past Stella's lips. "That's it."

She would invite June and her family to come here for a visit. And what better time than Christmas? That way they could enjoy the town's Christmas Eve celebration. Of course, she would have to invite Noah back as well, but the cabin was plenty big enough.

Christmas in Evergreen Point. What could be more perfect? It was the break from the norm that they all needed. Oh, she couldn't wait to float the suggestion by Noah.

Christmas in Evergreen Point

But what if June refused? Stella's heart sank. Well, she would have to deal with that when—*if* it happened. For now, she could begin planning, not that there was a lot to do. The cabin was already decorated, so it wouldn't take any time to get the rooms ready. Her biggest hurdle would be getting more food, but that shouldn't pose too much of a problem, considering she still had a few weeks before the holiday.

Oh, this was exciting! She could hardly keep herself from running upstairs to tell Noah about it right now. Somehow, she managed though. Luckily, she didn't have too long to wait since Noah trotted down the stairs about five minutes later.

"How is your sister?" Stella asked cautiously.

He chuckled and shook his head. "Never could fool you." He scratched his chin. "Everything is good."

"Well, I had an idea while you were reporting back to your sister. I was thinking about having you and June's family here for Christmas. What do you think?"

She watched as he frowned, his expression reminding her so much of his father that it made the back of her throat ache. Dale always looked like that whenever he was debating something. The same furrowed brow and creased forehead. Same dark hair and eyes.

"I don't have a problem with it," Noah admitted. "And I think June might be open to it." His gazed locked on hers. "But you're going to have to ask her yourself. I'm tired of being the go-between. You two need to work this out."

Sighing, Stella nodded. "That can only happen if she actually takes my call."

"She will. She's calmer now."
Stella smiled, hoping her son was right.

CHAPTER 18

That night, Stella and Noah went into town for dinner at one of the local restaurants, where they both enjoyed burgers, fries, and beer. Several locals stopped by their table to say hello throughout the meal.

"Everyone is so friendly here," Noah said. "It's nothing like the city."

"It's nice, right?" Stella asked.

"It is." He smiled at her. "I see why you like it here. I think coming here was a great decision on your part."

"You do?" She was surprised but grateful to hear it.

"Yes."

He got that faraway look in his eyes that he always did when he was plotting.

"What are you thinking?" she asked.

"Honestly, I'm thinking about checking out the real estate listings."

Her mouth fell open. "What?"

"Easy now," Noah said. "I was thinking about a vacation home … maybe. On the lake, if possible. One that the whole family could share and enjoy."

While she was happy that he liked the town, she wasn't sure how to feel about this. Money had nothing to do with it; Dale had left plenty for them. She was more concerned about making too rash of a decision.

"Honey, if a vacation home is something you're interested in, that's fine, but don't you think you should shop around?" she asked. "There might even be some options closer to home."

Frowning, Noah shook his head. "Why bother? You love it here. You've made friends here. The town is great. Why would you need to look anywhere else?"

Her heart kicked in her chest. "You mean a vacation home for *me*?"

"Well, yeah. If you wanted, we could go into it together but I figured you have all that money dad left you. It would be a good investment. And who knows? Maybe you'll eventually retire here."

Stunned, Stella sat back against the cushioned booth. A vacation home here in Evergreen Point? The idea had never even crossed her mind. She couldn't believe Noah had suggested such a thing. What's more, she couldn't believe how happy the idea made her. She *was* happy here.

A tiny thrill zipped through her as she began to allow herself to believe this could actually happen. But what about June? How would she feel about this?

As if he read her mind, Noah said, "I wouldn't bring it up to June just yet. It would probably be better to wait until after she visits."

If she visited, Stella thought but kept it to herself.

"What do you think?" Noah asked. "I could check into it. Contact a realtor."

"I-I think it's a great idea, but maybe we should think about it for a few days, at least. I don't want to jump the gun."

"Mom." Noah leaned forward. "Don't let June's bratty attitude deter you. You don't need our permission for something like this." He paused. "You really haven't thought about this at all before now?"

Shaking her head, she said, "It never crossed my mind." She realized that wasn't completely true. "Well, I mean, maybe in passing while out walking, but I never truly considered it." She looked at her son in awe. "I *could* do this, couldn't I?"

"Yes, you could."

"Well, how about that?"

Noah finished his beer and signaled to the waitress for another round, while Stella let herself get lost in the dream of becoming a part of this amazing town.

The waitress appeared with fresh drinks and asked if they wanted dessert. Noah ordered a piece of chocolate cake for them to split. Thinking about all of the Christmas cookies at the cabin, Stella started to protest, but then figured what the hell. Noah was leaving tomorrow so she might as well enjoy this time with him.

"Well, hey there, Ms. Stella."

She looked up to see Howie coming towards their table. "Howie, hi! Are you by yourself? Would you like to join us?"

"Thanks, but Celia is meeting me here." He nodded at Noah. "Hello, young man."

"Hi. Um, your daughter owns the rental agency, right?"

"She does."

"Is it just the rental side of the business she's involved in, or does she also deal with sales?"

Howie's gray eyebrows rose. "You thinking about buying around here?"

Noah nodded. "Mom and I were just entertaining the idea of a vacation home. We haven't decided for sure just yet, but I figured it couldn't hurt to look around and see what's available."

"Well now. That's wonderful news. I'm sure Celia could get you whatever info you need."

Celia appeared just then and Howie told her about their interest in available properties. She was delighted, of course, and very eager to help. She said she would check the listings and email them.

Once they were alone again, Stella said to Noah, "So much for thinking about it for a few days."

Noah laughed. "We *are* thinking about it. We're just shopping around to see what's available." He shrugged. "Who knows? We might not like anything right now. We'll just have to see."

"You young people just zoom right on ahead with things, don't you?"

"I don't see the problem?"

She blew out a breath. "Just give your old mother a little bit of time to catch up, okay?"

The waitress appeared with the bill and Noah, against her protests, paid it. Then they headed back to the cabin.

CHAPTER 19

Sunday morning Stella found an email in her inbox from Celia telling her that there weren't any houses on the lake currently up for sale, but she did supply a list of several houses nearby and closer to town. She also said that she would keep an ear out and let Stella know the second she heard of any newly listed properties.

Even though she knew she wanted a house on the water, Stella browsed through the list anyway. While there were some nice, charming houses, none of them caught her eye enough to make her reconsider. Noah agreed that she should hold out for what she really wanted.

She still couldn't believe she was considering this. The idea wasn't brand new; she and Dale had discussed buying a vacation home at some point. But after he passed, it didn't occur to her that she could still buy one on her own.

When Noah went upstairs to pack his things and get a shower before his drive home, Stella poured a fresh mug of coffee and took it, along with a thick blanket out onto the back porch. It was cold, but she made a cozy nest for herself in one of the lounge chairs and looked out over the water. It was so peaceful here.

She let her mind wander, imagining how much livelier it would be in the warmer months with the houses full of people spilling out into the water. She could almost hear the laughter of the children splashing in the lake and smell the smoke wafting from fire pits in the evenings.

The door behind her opened and Noah stepped out onto the porch. "What in the world are you sitting out here for? It's freezing!"

"It's not so bad."

"Not so bad? I've been out here ten seconds and already I can't feel my nose. Please, let's go back inside."

Chuckling at his dramatics, she followed him inside. He poured himself more coffee and they sat in front of the fireplace.

"You really do love it here, don't you?" Noah asked.

She cast a quizzical look at him. "Was I that bad before?"

Immediately shaking his head, he said, "Not bad. Just sad. Lost." He stared into the flames. "It's like you found that missing part of yourself here."

"Maybe I did," she murmured.

"Mmhmm," her son hummed.

She recognized that sound. "What? What is it? What are you thinking?"

"Nothing."

But there was a hint of sadness in the word. Stella wasn't quite sure what to make of it, but it was not 'nothing' as he claimed. Was it because he would miss her when she visited here? Was he worried she would sell the house in which he'd grown up?

"Well, I guess I should be heading out," Noah said as he got to his feet. "I'm glad I came."

"Me too." Stella followed him to the door, where she kissed his cheek. "Drive safely and let me know when you get to your apartment."

"I will." He enveloped her in a hug. "I love you, Mom. Take care of yourself."

"I will," she parroted.

"And call Junie." He frowned slightly. "But remember, don't tell her about your plans to buy a house here. Not yet."

"I won't. I don't think she's ready for that yet. I agree with you that she should visit first."

"All right. I'm off."

Stella walked out onto the front porch to see him off. Waving as he drove away, she sighed. Now she needed to patch things up with June. Hopefully, her daughter would be a little more receptive now that Noah had scoped out the situation for her.

"Good morning," Caleb said as he crossed his yard to hers. "I see Noah left. Did you have a nice visit?"

"Yes. It was too short, of course. I didn't realize how much I missed him until I just watched him drive away."

"Did I pass the test?" he asked, barely containing a chuckle. "Does he agree I'm not a danger to your safety?"

"You did. The whole town did, actually."

"Really? Are we that charming, or is he just easy to please?"

Stella laughed. "Both, I think. Come inside for some coffee. It's cold today."

Caleb gave a whistle as he followed her inside. Boomer came trotting through the door after them. Stella closed the door, and then went into the kitchen to prepare more coffee.

"You'll never guess what Noah suggested," she said as she scooped coffee into the French press. "He suggested I buy a vacation home here."

"You're kidding. Wow. I guess this place did charm him. Are you going to do it?"

"I think I might. That is, if anything becomes available that I like. Right now, the only properties for sale are closer to town. I'd rather be on the water, if possible."

Caleb smiled. "I guess we charmed you, too. Wait a minute. You've already looked?"

"Yes. Celia sent me some links this morning."

"You move fast."

She shrugged. "Not me. Noah. We were at dinner last night and so were your dad and Celia, so Noah brought it up with her." She shook her head slowly. "I still haven't decided anything for sure. While my son likes to plow full-steam ahead whenever he gets an idea, I prefer to take my time and make sure it's something I really want."

Arching a brow, he said, "So you *aren't* sure you want a second home here?"

She poured the boiling water over the coffee grounds and set the timer before sitting down at the table with him. "I think I am. I love it here. It's just a big decision to make, and I'm not used to making those on my own." She bit her lower lip, thinking, and then added, "I mean, Dale and I were talking about the possibility of buying a vacation home at some point. I just never thought I'd be doing it without him."

Caleb nodded. "I understand. But it doesn't sound like you're doing it on your own. Noah is helping you."

Nodding, she brushed her hair back over her shoulder. "That's true. I didn't think of it like that."

"I know it's not exactly the same; Noah is your son, not your husband."

"Huh," she said as she sat back.

Caleb had a point. Even though it felt like it sometimes, she wasn't alone. Not completely. She still had her children to help her make decisions when she needed it. That was comforting. And a surprise. She hadn't realized that she needed that kind of comfort. Maybe comfort wasn't the right word. Security. Yes, that sounded better.

"Have you talked to your daughter about it?" Caleb asked.

Eyes going wide, she quickly said, "Oh, no. She's barely talking to me as it is."

"Ah, I see."

"What?"

"It's her opinion that's making you so hesitant. You're worried about upsetting her further."

A bark of laughter burst from her. "I think everything I say or do, especially these days, upsets her in some way. June has always been … high-strung. Dale could always handle her better than I could."

It was true. June was a daddy's girl through and through. It had always amazed Stella at how easily he could navigate her tantrums.

The timer went off and Stella poured him a mug and topped off her own. "Do you think it's too soon for me to make such a big change?"

Surprise shuttered over his face. "I don't think my opinion matters very much."

"Sure, it does. What if I were your dad three years ago."

A shadow of grief passed briefly over his face before he said, "Dad told you about Mom then?"

She nodded.

"I absolutely would have supported his decision. This hypothetical is a moot point anyway. My dad hates change. Hell, I can't even recall the last time he took a vacation. Also, your daughter sounds nothing like me, so there's that, too."

"Very true." She smirked and said, "Although, you can be quite moody at times. Kind of like her."

He groaned and dragged a hand down his face. "Now you sound like my sister. I think moodiness is a trait of all writers though, isn't it? Nobody likes being distracted when they're in the zone."

"Speaking of your writing, how dare you not tell me you're a famous mystery writer! I thought we were friends."

His eyes darted down to the mug in his hands, and if Stella wasn't mistaken, color bloomed in his cheeks. When he spoke, his voice had lowered a couple of octaves. "We are friends. I'm sorry I didn't tell you, but it's nice meeting people as myself and not C.J. Abrahams. I know that probably doesn't make sense to you."

Tilting her head sideways, she searched his face. For what, she wasn't sure. When his eyes came back up to meet hers, she felt the air lodge in her chest. Suddenly uncomfortable, she pushed her chair back and stood up. Heart pumping, she went to the sink and dumped her coffee before rinsing the cup. Heat crept into her own cheeks as she shifted her weight, trying to ease the tension tugging on her lower abdomen.

What was happening to her? If she wasn't mistaken, her body was reacting to Caleb. Oh, my. Surely, she wasn't attracted to him. Was she?

A cold wave of guilt washed over her, dousing the burn that had been building inside her. This was inappropriate. Dale had not been gone that long.

Two years wasn't long enough. Was it?

Behind her, Caleb cleared his throat. "Thank you for the coffee. I should get back to work."

Without turning around, she responded, "O-okay. I'll see you later then."

"Sure."

Once she was alone, Stella sank into her kitchen chair again. Leaning forward, she covered her face with both hands as guilt overwhelmed her. She loved Dale. How in the world could she possibly be thinking about another man in a sexual way? It had barely been two years since she lost Dale. What kind of wife did this make her, if after twenty-five years of marriage, she was attracted to the first man she met?

Crying freely now, she rested her head on the table in front of her as she told herself she was just lonely. Caleb was the first person since Dale who had offered any form of male companionship, so she was latching onto it. The companionship. Sitting by the fire, sharing meals, having conversations with, and discussing her life choices with.

She gasped softly. That's it. She was asking his opinion about her buying a house here on the lake as if he were Dale. She wasn't sure when it happened, but she'd subconsciously put Caleb in Dale's vacant companion slot in her life.

Well, she would just have to be more careful from here on out. There was no way she was trying to replace Dale in her life. There was no way she could. Her husband would always have a special place in her heart. She was not ready to move on from him or their marriage yet.

Was she?

CHAPTER 20

Later that night, June called as Stella was heating up leftovers for dinner. Already feeling anxious, Stella stared at her phone, debating on whether to answer it or not. She wasn't sure she was up for this conversation right now. Finally, she pressed answer.

"Hello, sweetheart."

"Hi, Mom." An awkward silence dangled between them. "So, your visit with Noah went well? It sounds like he had a great time in your little town."

Stella's heart stuttered at the barely suppressed resentment in her daughter's voice.

"We had a lovely time," she said. "So lovely, in fact, it gave me an idea." Here goes nothing. "What if you guys came here for Christmas? The town puts on a wonderful Christmas Eve celebration."

When June didn't say anything right away, Stella pushed ahead and told her all about the festivities. She did not, however, mention a thing about a vacation home yet. Baby steps.

"I don't understand," June said. "I thought you went there to get away from all that over-the-top Christmas stuff."

"Honestly, I thought I did, too. But it's … different here. It's nothing like Christmas in the city. It's magical. I would love to share it with you and the kids. Speaking of the kids, how are they?"

"They're fine." June sighed. "I don't know, Mom. I'm not sure packing up the kids and being away from home on Christmas is the best idea."

"Well, it's up to you, of course, but I would love to spend Christmas with all of you."

"Since when? I thought you needed a break from us?"

Stella sucked in a breath. "Honey, you know that's not true. My coming here had nothing to with you and everything to do with me. I'm sorry if you took it that way. Just consider it, please. The kids will love it. I promise. I got a huge tree and the trimmings already. Ask Noah. I've turned the cabin into a mini winter wonderland. All that's missing is all of you."

June was silent again, and Stella could picture her gnawing on her lower lip while she considered the proposal.

Finally, June said, "I'll have to ask Will and the kids."

Grinning now, Stella replied, "Of course. Just let me know, so I can do the shopping for the big dinner in time."

"What is the name of this place again?"

"Evergreen Point."

"Okay. I'll talk to Will. You sound … good. I'm glad."

Stella's heart swelled. "Thank you, honey. I feel better."

"I'm happy for you. Look, I have to run. It sounds like I'm needed upstairs."

"Go. Take care of the kids. Give them hugs from me."

"I will. Love you."

Eyes watering, Stella said hoarsely, "I love you, too. Talk to you soon."

Feeling much better, Stella dug into her lasagna. In her heart, she knew that her family would be here for Christmas. Smiling, she sent a text to Noah telling him that she'd spoken with June. He sent back a thumb's up emoji, making her laugh.

She finished her dinner, cleaned her dishes, and then went into the living room to find a movie to watch on TV. She snuggled under the blanket as the wind picked up outside, indicating another front was moving into the area. It wasn't long before she fell asleep.

The sound of her phone woke her up some time in the night. Groggy, she checked it. It was a little after three in the morning. There was a text message from Caleb on her phone asking if she was okay. It was only then that she realized the cabin was lit only by the glow of the fire.

She got up and stoked the fire, adding another log, before she replied to his message saying she was fine. He said the storm was supposed to continue for the next day or so and to let him know if she needed anything.

Since the power was out, she decided to sleep on the sofa in front of the fire. She used her phone as a flashlight to go upstairs and change into some flannel pajamas. Then she went back downstairs and resumed her spot on the sofa and fell back to sleep to the sound of the crackling fire against a backdrop of howling wind.

The next morning, the snow and wind outside still raged. Stella understood now why Caleb kept the wood pile fully stocked. She couldn't imagine how cold the cabin would be without a fire. After tending said fire, she went into the kitchen to try to figure out what she was going to do about coffee.

A bang on the door made her jump. She raced to it and yanked it open. Boomer and Caleb both rushed inside and shaking off snow.

"Oh, my goodness!" she exclaimed. "Let me get some towels!"

She shot up the stairs lightning fast and returned with an armful of towels. Caleb stripped off his poncho.

"Thanks," he said, taking a towel and wiping his face and arms. "I think Boomer is worse. Boomer, come boy!"

The dog was already in front of the fire but came trotting dutifully back to his owner, who Stella just noticed was carrying a cooler.

"Boom, sit," Caleb said, then began to dry the dog.

"What's in the cooler?" Stella asked as she helped wipe the dog down.

"You're going to love me," Caleb said with crooked smile.

Spine stiffening, Stella forced herself to relax. "Oh, really?"

Once Boomer was dried and back in front of the fire, Caleb carried the cooler into the kitchen. Curious,

Stella followed and waited patiently for the big reveal. She gasped when he pulled out a big thermos.

"Is that what I think it is?" she asked, already moving to get some mugs.

"Yes, ma'am." Caleb pulled out a brown paper bag next. "And muffins."

After taking the first sip of hot coffee, Stella said, "I cannot believe you went out in this storm! But thank you."

"I didn't. I have a fireplace grill, so I was able to boil some water and heat up some day-old muffins."

"I had no idea such a thing existed. What a great idea."

Caleb nodded. "Yeah. I don't think any of the other cabins have one, but since I'm here year-round, it made sense to purchase one." He paused and sipped his coffee. "Once the worst is over, I can get the generator going until the power comes back on."

Stella got a couple of paper plates for the muffins and they sat down at the table to eat.

"This might be the best cup of coffee I've ever had," she said.

Caleb laughed. "So, did Noah get home okay?"

She nodded. "He did. Oh, and I invited June and her family to come for Christmas. She said she would think about it."

"At least she didn't say no."

"At least. She sounded hesitant though. I'm just glad the call ended on good terms this time."

"I take it you didn't mention the vacation home?"

She shook her head. "Oh, no. Not yet. I'm saving that for later. Besides, I still haven't decided for sure.

There's no use in possibly upsetting her even more for no reason."

"You will when something you like becomes available."

"Maybe."

It was easy to be noncommittal when there was nothing she liked. It would be harder when—*if* she found a place that fit her needs. Looking around them, she silently wished this place would go up for sale.

Her gaze went back to Caleb. Having him next door was an added perk. Just look at how convenient it was this morning. Although, if she bought a place, she would make sure she would be prepared like he was. She made a mental note to put fireplace grill and a generator at the top of her shopping list if she did buy a lake house.

"There's a lot of thinking going on over there," Caleb said. "Care to share?"

She sighed. "I'm just thinking about possibilities. What I should really be thinking about is my shopping list for Christmas dinner."

Caleb nodded. "Do you usually have dinner on Christmas Eve or Christmas Day? I know everyone has their own preference. My family usually has Christmas Day dinner because we eat in town on Christmas Eve."

"Oh. We usually get together Christmas Eve. Is there a big dinner in town or something similar to the last time? You know, food trucks and such."

"There are some food trucks during the day, but in the evening there's a big buffet set up. Everyone brings a few dishes, and there are several families who bring turkeys, hams, ducks, and the like. There are also lots of lasagnas. A little something for everyone."

Stunned, Stella stared at him. "The whole town eats together?"

He nodded. "Or they pack up food and take it home to eat. It's a great way for those less fortunate to enjoy a delicious Christmas meal."

"How lovely." She smiled. "You know, the longer I'm here, the harder it is going to be to leave."

"Then don't. I'm sure you could extend your rental. The season doesn't start to pick up until May around here."

"I can't do that. I promised my kids I would be home for New Year's."

He shrugged. "Okay then. It was just a thought."

And what a wonderful one at that. Gazing down at her coffee, Stella felt a small tug of regret in her chest. She was beginning to realize it was going to be difficult to leave this place.

"Refill?" Caleb asked and she nodded. "Since we're stuck inside today, how about some cards or a board game or something? Unless you want me to go."

"Oh, no! You can stay, but I don't have any games."

He stood up. "Every cabin has a game stash."

She watched as he went to a small closet built into the base of the stairs. He opened the door and gave a small cheer before turning back to her.

"I told you. Everyone around here keeps a rainy-day stash. So, cards or a board game?"

"You pick."

"Rummy it is then!" He came back with cards and got busy shuffling while she cleared the table of their breakfast mess.

He dealt the cards and they played throughout the morning. After a quick lunch of simple sandwiches, they switched over to Battleship. By the time dinnertime rolled around, the weather had quieted, so they switched locations to his house to heat up some dinner over the fire. After that, Stella returned to her cabin to sleep.

"What a lovely day," she said to herself as she drifted off to sleep.

CHAPTER 21

The storm was still raging the next morning. Caleb appeared at her door once more with coffee and muffins. They enjoyed an easy breakfast together and then decided on a board game to pass the time.

"It's been a while since I played Monopoly," Stella admitted as they set up the board. "How much longer do you think the storm is going to last?"

"The weather report said things should start calming down tomorrow."

She nodded and turned her focus to the game. They chatted amiably while they played. Caleb ended up winning but Stella had fun. It was nice to have company while the storm howled outside. It was also nice to have someone who was willing to go outside and get more firewood, so she didn't have to get cold and wet. Though she did feel slightly guilty about that.

For lunch, Caleb found a pot with a long handle in one of the cabinets. Stella got some leftover stew from the freezer and he was able to hold the pot over the fire to thaw and warm it up enough for them to eat.

"My goodness," Stella said. "I guess I should take notes on how to survive storms around here."

They both laughed and then finished their stew. Stella rinsed the dishes and left them in the sink. When she turned around, she saw that Caleb was pulling out his laptop.

"Do you mind if I write for a little bit?" he asked. "Even though it's storming, I still have a deadline to meet."

"Go right ahead. I can entertain myself for a little while. Um, would you like to use one of the bedrooms?"

He shook his head as he set up his laptop and notebooks on the kitchen table. "I'm good here. That is, if you don't mind?"

"I don't mind at all. Do you have enough battery?"

"I have an extra one."

"Oh, okay." She found her tablet and checked the battery, grateful to find that it was at sixty percent. "I'll just read."

She settled on the sofa with her tablet and Boomer, who jumped up to lie beside her with his head on her leg. She stroked his head as she began to read and Caleb began to type. To her surprise, the steady sound of the clicking keys was quite soothing.

Every once in a while, Caleb would mutter under his breath and she would just smile to herself. She'd never been in the presence of a real writer at work before. Just wait until she told Noah that she was sitting feet away while C.J. Abrahams wrote his latest book.

Caleb sighed loudly and sat back and stretched in his chair. "What are you smiling about over there?" he asked.

"Oh, nothing. Just thinking about what my son will say when I tell him I got to see you hard at work on your latest book."

"Not as glamorous as you envisioned, huh?"

"I don't know. It's pretty much what I expected, except I did picture you drinking a glass of whisky or something while you write."

He chuckled. "Honestly, I wouldn't turn down a glass right about now. It might help me finally hash out this scene."

"Would you like me to pour you one?" She set her tablet down and got to her feet. "It's not like you're driving anywhere anytime soon."

"No, that's okay." He turned back to his computer and frowned at the screen.

She went into the kitchen to pour herself a glass of tea. Since he had resumed typing furiously, she didn't bother to ask if he wanted one and just set a glass on the table next to him. She was rewarded with a gratuitous grunt. Smiling to herself, she went back to her book.

Time passed quickly in companionable silence, before they knew it, it was time for dinner. Stella had finished her book and Caleb snapped his laptop closed with a groan.

"Hungry?" she asked.

Nodding, he rose and stretched, raising his arms above his head. "I'm starving actually. I didn't even realize how late it is. Sorry about that."

"No need to apologize. I finished my book, and it was nice to have company."

She went into the kitchen to make them some sandwiches.

"What were you reading?" he asked.

"Oh. It was Southern Noir novel about two lifelong friends who find themselves back home after one of their friends was found dead in the swamp."

"Huh. I was expecting you to say a romance novel."

"How stereotypical of you, Mr. Abrahams."

"I didn't mean it to be. Romance is the top selling genre in the industry. Even I read the occasional romance novel." He laughed when he saw the surprised look on her face. "What can I say? I like staying on top of what resonates with readers."

"But I thought you wrote mysteries. Wait, are you about to confess that you secretly write romance novels under a penname?"

Raising an eyebrow, he asked, "And if I did, would that really be that shocking?"

Blinking, she exclaimed, "Yes. You don't seem the type."

"Now who's being stereotypical? Do you have any idea how many men write romance and erotica under a female pseudonym?"

"Really?"

He nodded. "Really. I, however, am not one of them though."

She tossed a dish towel at him. "You had me going for a minute!"

He grinned. "I know. Hey, more power to those men who do though. A buddy of mine doesn't even bother with a pseudonym. He has quite the following."

"That's interesting."

"I take it you've never read a romance written by a man?"

"No, I haven't. I usually just buy what's popular."

"Most people do."

She didn't miss the disapproving tone in his voice. It was subtle but it was there.

"Is there something wrong with that?" she asked.

"Not at all. You have no idea what you're missing out on though. I'm friends with a lot of Indie writers. Some of them write better stories than most traditionally published writers like myself."

"Huh. Honestly, I've never even thought about it. Maybe I'll broaden my horizons."

"You should. I think you'll be surprised." He frowned and then reached for his bag. "In fact, I think I have one with me." He pulled a book from the side pocket of his bag. "Here. Try it."

She set his sandwich in front of him before taking the book from him and reading the back cover.

"Sounds interesting," she said, sitting down. "Okay. After dinner I'll give it a go. But what about you? What will you do?"

He held up his e-reader. "I have one for myself."

They continued to chat about books while they ate. Then Caleb braved the storm to take Boomer outside. Stella helped wipe the dog down when they came back inside. Then they spent the rest of the evening in front of the fire reading quietly together. Stella almost felt like a kid again using a flashlight to read.

She had to admit that the book Caleb lent her was one of the funniest rom-coms she had ever read. She found herself laughing out loud several times. There were also several steamy parts that had her blushing. She wasn't used to reading such scenes with a man who wasn't her husband sitting in such close proximity.

When she couldn't stop yawning, Stella set the book down and announced she was going to bed. Caleb stood and called out to Boomer but the dog didn't budge from his cozy spot in front of the fire.

"It's still snowing pretty bad," Stella said. "Why don't you two just sleep here instead?" Seeing the surprised look on his face, she quickly added, "There are three other bedrooms available in this cabin."

"Thanks, but he needs to go out one last time anyway."

"Are you sure? Won't it be cold at your place? You've been here all day."

"I'll be fine. It won't take long for the bedroom to heat up once I get the fire going. Thank you for letting us hang out here all day." He went to the door and slid his arms into his coat. "You were right earlier; it was nice to have some company."

She smiled. "You're very welcome."

"Okay, Boomer. Come on, boy!"

Caleb rolled his eyes as the dog took his time standing and stretching before finally trotting to the door. When Caleb opened it, Boomer looked up at him with an appalled look on his face, making Stella laugh and shake her head. She didn't blame him for not wanting to go out in the cold, wet mess.

"Good night," Caleb said as he ushered Boomer outside.

"Good night."

Stella peeked her head out the door and watched the two of them race through the yard to the house next door. Then she closed hers and made her way up the stairs to bed.

CHAPTER 22

The next afternoon June called to say that she and her family were coming to Evergreen Point for Christmas. Ecstatic, Stella flew into planning mode. She made a grocery list, but unfortunately that was all the weather was going to allow for the day. Once the storm was gone, she would head into town and buy food, new sheets for the beds, and anything else she added to her list.

For now, she was stuck inside. Thankfully, the power came back on so she would no longer need to rely on Caleb for coffee and hot food. She had to admit that she would miss his company though. But now that the power was back, she knew he would be busy at his laptop again.

At least she had the TV to keep her company. First thing the next morning she would head into town and tackle that shopping list.

Noah called to check in on the vacation home situation. Unfortunately, no new properties had hit the market. Stella was secretly relieved because once she found a suitable house, she would have to approach June with the idea.

"I don't understand," Howie said when she told him about her hesitation. "You're an adult; June is an adult. What either of you do with your own money or lives is not any of the other's business."

"That's true, but …"

"But what?" Howie asked. "Honey, you lost your husband. If buying a vacation home will make you happy, then do it. It shouldn't matter what anyone else thinks."

Stella swallowed hard as she digested his words. She knew he meant well, but she found herself feeling like a chastised child. He was right though. It was *her* life. Why was she so worried about how June felt about it? If Dale were still here, she wouldn't give June's attitude a second thought.

But Dale wasn't here. And June was taking his loss the hardest.

"My head understands what you're saying," Stella said. "But my heart is having a tough time with it. June is struggling with so much right now."

Howie reached across the counter and took her by the hand. "Stella, I know exactly what you mean, but I'm here to tell you that giving your daughter this power over you and your life is not going to help either one of you move on."

Nodding, Stella said, "That's why I'm here in Evergreen Point."

"That was a great first step to moving on for you. Now you need to *keep* moving on. Your daughter will struggle with it, and so will your son, but you need to heal in your own way. Let them find theirs. And *not* by becoming overprotective of you and your life. June

127

needs to find her own way to deal that doesn't involve you."

"That sounds kind of harsh."

Howie smiled. "The truth usually does." He gave her hand a reassuring squeeze. "I know it's hard."

"Thank you." While she meant it, she also couldn't help but feel a bit resentful as well. Who was this man to tell her how to parent her own child?

"How about we get your purchases loaded into your car?" Howie suggested.

She nodded. "Okay."

Once everything was loaded in her car, Howie gave her a hug. "I'm glad you're thinking about sticking around. You fit in well here. Please, don't let your daughter guilt you out of it."

"Like you're trying to guilt me *into* it?"

He chuckled. "Touché, Ms. Stella."

As she drove back to her cabin, she thought about her conversation with Howie. She couldn't imagine poor June living a life mired in grief. That possibility broke her heart. Surely, she could help her daughter learn to cope with her father's loss.

But was it her responsibility? Maybe Howie was right. Maybe she should step back and let June find her own way, even if it did make her mother's heart ache.

She pulled up to the cabin and cut the engine before sitting back. Just the sight of this place brought her peace. She knew in her heart that this was where she was meant to be right now. That this was where she needed to be to heal. To move on. She could only hope it might offer her children the same over time.

Her worries and anxiety settled, reassuring her that Dale would agree.

"You would have loved this place," she whispered.

It was true. Dale had been talking for years about finding a lake house to spend their retirement. So, in part, purchasing a house here was as much for him as it was for herself. An ode to his dream. The realization made her smile. She had to do it, and she wasn't going to let June guilt her out of taking her life back.

CHAPTER 23

With Christmas only five days away, Stella was a blur of activity making sure the house was cleaned and ready, the presents wrapped and under the tree, and most of the baking was done. The children would want to help bake the sugar cookies for Santa, of course, so she would wait on those.

That afternoon the sound of Boomer barking announced her family's arrival. Stella rushed out to the porch to greet them.

Boomer and the kids were already well on their way to becoming the best of friends, making Stella's smile widen even more.

"You got a dog?" June asked as she got out of the car.

"Not mine. He's the neighbor's, remember?"

"Ah, yes, the neighbor." June said tightly as she came up the steps and embraced her. "I've missed you. It's so good to see you."

Squeezing her daughter tightly, Stella said, "Me, too."

Releasing her, June stepped back. "Okay kids! It's time to unpack your things."

Reluctantly, they plodded back to the car. Not easily deterred, Boomer pranced at their heels. Stella led them all inside and directed them to their rooms upstairs. When she inquired after Noah, June told her that he'd stopped in town for something.

Once all of the luggage was taken upstairs and unpacked, the children oohed and awed over the tree. Even Will complimented it.

"It is beautiful," June admitted. Taking in the rest of the cabin, she added, "All of it is. You've made this place feel like a home, not a rental."

Smiling, Stella said, "Well, it has been my home for the past several weeks."

June's face soured, making Stella's chest tighten. Why couldn't she just be happy that her mother was happy for once?

"This place is pretty amazing," Will said. "I bet it would be even better during the spring and summer."

"Oh, you haven't seen anything yet," Stella said. She went to the back door and parted the drapes, revealing the picturesque lake. "Isn't it beautiful? And wait until you see the town. Everyone is so friendly. It's just lovely, and boy, do they know how to throw a party. You'll see on Christmas Eve."

The kids asked a bunch of questions about the party, and Stella told them they would all have to wait and see because she'd never been herself. However, she did tell them about the Welcome Christmas celebration she had attended.

"It all sounds so charming," Will said. "I can't wait."

"What about Christmas Eve dinner?" June asked. "We're still doing that, right?" When she saw her mother's hesitation, she snapped, "It's tradition. We always eat Christmas dinner on Christmas Eve."

"Honey," Will said, his apologetic eyes meeting Stella's.

"Well, June," Stella said calmly, "We also usually have Christmas at home, but here we are. Besides, what can it hurt changing things up for one year?"

Boomer, who had been with the kids this whole time, gave a low whine and came to Stella's side. He nudged her leg, making her look down at him with a smile. She stroked his head.

"I thought you said he was the neighbor's dog," June pointed out. "He seems awfully comfortable here."

Will placed a hand on June's arm and she shrugged it off.

Thankfully, the sound of footsteps outside created a distraction. Stella turned to the door to greet her son as it opened.

"Hey, Mom," Noah said, dragging his suitcase behind him. Almost immediately, he picked up on the tension in the room and his smile fell. "Everything okay here?" he asked, his eyes darting to his sister.

"Everything is just fine," June hissed.

Stella offered him a wobbly smile. "How was your trip? June said you had to go into town for something?"

He nodded. "The trip was uneventful, and as for my errand, you'll just have to wait and see."

She didn't know what to make of the mischievous twinkle in his eyes. She could only hope that whatever his surprise errand was, it didn't have anything to do with her purchasing a house here. Given June's prickly demeanor, Stella still had a long way to go before she could bring up that subject.

While Noah took his belongings upstairs, Stella put some water on to boil for coffee and tea. Then she arranged some cookies on a platter and poured two glasses of milk for the kids. By the time the coffee and tea were both steeping, Noah had returned downstairs. Stella called everyone into the kitchen.

"I figured you all could use an afternoon treat," she said as they all sat down at the table.

When Boomer sat down in front of her and held up a paw, she automatically turned to the cabinet that housed his treats.

"Grandma, can I give him a treat?" Lizzie asked.

"Me too!" Her younger brother, Logan, exclaimed.

"Okay, but just one a piece. We don't want to ruin his dinner."

She gave the kids the treats and Boomer sat up on his haunches for one and then laid down for the other.

"Wash your hands, please," June said, her nose crinkled in disgust.

The kids obliged and then returned to their seats to eat their own treats. Stella brought the cream and sugar to the table before pouring everyone's drinks.

"So, Junie," Noah said, "What do you think of the place so far? Isn't it great?"

"It's a cabin in the winter," she replied. Catching the hopeful look on Stella's face, she added, "But somehow Mom made it feel warm and cozy. Like a home."

Touched, Stella smiled at her daughter.

Noah turned to her. "So, Mom, what have you been up to since I've been gone?"

"Oh, the usual. Well, there was a storm."

She proceeded to tell them about losing power and Caleb coming to her rescue with fresh, hot coffee. Noah was intrigued by the fireplace grill. Stella silently begged him with her eyes not to mention the possibility of buying one for their lake house. Thankfully, he seemed to understand.

"I'm excited for this Christmas Eve celebration," he said. "How about you, kids?"

They both exclaimed in agreement, making everyone laugh.

June looked at her brother. "Did you know we aren't having dinner on Christmas Eve like we usually do?"

Noah's eyes flitted briefly to their mother before he answered cautiously, "I did not."

"Apparently, we're going to eat in town with a bunch of strangers instead," June said.

Taking a deep breath, Stella said, "We'll have our family dinner on Christmas Day. I want the kids to have the full experience of a magical Christmas in town."

"Just the kids?" Noah teased.

"Well, I would enjoy celebrating with my friends," Stella admitted.

Scowling, June asked, "Then why are we here if you would rather spend the holiday with your new *friends*?"

She had practically spat the word.

Stella sighed, and Noah said, "Stop it, Junie. Can't you see Mom is trying to share the holiday with *all* of us? What's the harm in that?"

His sister's eyes turned glassy and she excused herself from the table. She went to the door, grabbed her coat, and went outside, leaving the rest of them sitting in heavy silence.

"Why is Momma mad?" Lizzie asked.

Will sighed. "She's not mad, sweetie. She just misses Grandpa."

The little girl's eyes dropped to her lap. "Me, too."

Her younger brother nodded in agreement.

"We all do," Stella said, her throat thick with withheld tears. "That's why I thought having Christmas here would be fun. You know, something new."

"I think Grandpa would like this place," Logan said.

Stella's heart warmed. "I think so, too."

"I agree," Noah said. "Now, how about we get our coats and go for a little walk and check out the lake?"

The kids jumped out of their chairs and ran for the door. Once they were bundled up, Noah led them outside. Stella turned to Will.

"I'm sorry, Stella," he said. "June still misses Dale terribly. The holidays always seem to be the hardest."

Nodding, Stella said, "I know. That's exactly why I needed a change this year. I hoped it would help her as well."

"I think it will. It's just going to take some time." He smiled. "It's definitely done you some good. You seem happier."

"I am." She cringed. "It's hard to admit that without feeling guilty."

"Dale wouldn't want you to feel guilty; he would want you to be happy. To move on with your life. Speaking of moving on, when are we going to get meet this neighbor of yours?"

Blushing, Stella said, "It's not like that. Caleb is a great friend." She bit her lower lip. "I'm not sure if bringing him around June is a good idea."

"Well, you can't keep him hidden away forever."

"I'm not hiding him!" She laughed. "What a silly thing to say."

Will's laughter joined hers. "It feels that way. Noah really likes him, by the way. He said he's good guy."

While Stella appreciated him saying that, it also made her feel nervous. Knowing her son liked Caleb shouldn't make her so happy.

"That's nice to know," she admitted. Shifting in her seat, she asked, "So, should you go talk to June or should I?"

"I think it's your turn."

She nodded and went to get her coat before going outside in search of June. Stella found her standing on the shore of the lake. The faint chatter of Noah and the children floated back over the water to them. Stella spotted them farther down the shore.

"It *is* beautiful here," June said. "Even in this dreary, depressing weather."

"Yes, it is. I imagine it looks quite different in the height of summer."

June nodded. "Yeah. It's probably a lot louder, for sure. Busy."

"I would imagine so. I needed the quiet though."

"I'm sure that's my fault."

The sadness in her daughter's voice tugged on Stella's heart. She wished there was something she could do to help her.

"It's not," Stella softly. "I needed a break from my normal life, and believe it or not, it *has* been therapeutic."

June turned to her. "How can running away and hiding from your life help? Everything is still going to be the same when you go back. *If* you go back, that is."

"June, honey, of course I'm going back. It's my home."

"Is it? Because you seem to be settling in just fine here." June sighed. "And why wouldn't you? Look at this place. Plus, there aren't memories of Dad every time you turn around. It must be refreshing."

"It is. But it doesn't mean I miss him any less. I will always love your father. I'll always miss him, too. But I need to find a way to move on with my life."

June sniffled and nodded. "I know that. I do. I think I'm just scared."

"Of what?"

"Forgetting him. Losing you. I always knew I would have to face losing you guys eventually, but not this soon. He should still be here." Crying freely now, she shook her head. "No, not here. Home. We should all be home together."

"Oh, sweetheart," Stella said as she hugged her daughter to her. "I wish everything was the still the same, too, but it's not. And there's nothing we can do to change that."

"And yet that's exactly what you're trying to do. You're changing everything."

Well, she couldn't deny that. She *had* changed everything this year.

"June, this is only a change of pace. A *temporary* change of pace. Next year, we can go back to our old traditions. This is nothing but a vacation. Think of it like that. And a new experience for your children. Don't you think it will help them to have a break from the memories, too?"

June pulled back and nodded. "My head gets it, but my heart …"

Stella nodded. Hadn't she said something similar to Howie?

"I understand," she said. "We all do."

"But everyone else seems so well adjusted, and I feel so lost still. Left behind."

"Trust me when I say you're not alone. I can't tell you how many nights I've spent crying over your father."

June's face brightened. "Really? It seems like you don't miss him at all."

"Yes, really. Just ask Caleb. He was unlucky enough to witness one of my drunken breakdowns."

She hadn't meant to bring him into the conversation. The confession had just slipped out. Now, Stella held her breath, waiting for June to lash out again.

To her surprise, June said, "I'm glad he was there for you. I was worried about you being all alone here. Noah said Caleb is a good guy." June gave her a playful nudge. "*And* a famous author. I can't believe you didn't tell me."

"I swear I didn't know. I still can't believe it myself."

This time when June laughed, it was genuine. "Only you would befriend a famous author and never have read his books."

Stella shrugged. "What can I say? Life is funny sometimes. Have you read any of his books?"

"Uh, yeah. He's amazing. At least, his writing is. I'll have to reserve judgment on the man."

"Just try to go easy on him, okay? He's been a wonderful friend. His whole family has been great to me."

Tilting her head in consideration, June said, "Okay. I'll try. As long they understand they can't keep you."

This was the perfect opening for Stella to mention buying a vacation home here, but she chickened out. She didn't want to push June too much too soon.

Instead, she asked, "How about we go back inside now and enjoy that big fire?"

June put her arm through hers and they headed back to the cabin.

CHAPTER 24

Things between Stella and June seemed better after their talk. They got through the evening without any arguments or tense moments. After dinner, they cleaned the kitchen together while the kids turned on a Christmas movie.

Boomer hadn't left the kids' sides all day. Stella had sent Caleb a text, letting him know that Boomer was having a great time and was not a bother. Caleb thanked her and said he was going into town for the evening, so it worked out having Boomer at her place.

"Have you ever considered getting a dog?" Stella asked June quietly as she folded the dish towel.

Rolling her eyes, June replied, "That is the last thing we need. I would feel too bad leaving it alone all of the time. We're so busy."

"That's true. I didn't think about that."

Between work, school, and the various activities and sports the children were involved in, they spent little time at home. June was right; it wouldn't be fair to the dog.

"Have *you* ever thought about getting a dog?" June asked. "Boomer loves you, and you seem pretty fond of him."

Stella looked at Boomer as she considered the question. She had grown so used to having him around that she hadn't given a single thought to how much she was going to miss him when she left. Or how lonely home would suddenly feel.

"You know, I *was* thinking about it," she admitted. "I even mentioned it to Noah when he was here."

"You should think about it. I mean, you're all alone during the day in that house. It might be nice to have a companion." June smiled. "Just be prepared for your grandkids to want to spend every free moment at your house."

They laughed together as they went into the living room to join the rest of the family.

After the movie, everyone went upstairs to get ready for bed, while Stella put on her coat to take Boomer next door. She hadn't heard back from Caleb, so she sent him a quick text to let him know she was taking him to the house. Then she called softly to the dog as she opened the door.

They trekked next door and Stella opened the door for Boomer to go inside. As she turned to head down the porch steps, headlights lit up the small driveway. She waited for Caleb to park and get out of the car.

"Hey," she said.

"Hi. I was getting ready to text you and then I saw your text about bringing him home."

Smiling, Stella said, "Oh, he wanted to stay, and the kids wanted him to, but June thought they would rest better without him. I'm not sure that's true but who am I to undermine her parenting?"

"Are you two getting along better?"

"Yes, we had a talk. She's trying. How was your evening?"

"That's wonderful to hear," Caleb held the door for her, so she could enter. "I had dinner with Dad. It was nice."

"Oh, that's lovely. I wasn't sure if you went into town for business or pleasure."

"Well, it was a little bit of both. Would you like something to drink?"

"No, thank you. I'm going to head back home. It's been a good but tiring day."

"Okay. Thanks for looking out for my boy."

"You're welcome. Good night."

"Good night, Stella."

She let herself out and traipsed across the yard to her cabin. She went inside and quietly made her way upstairs. Smiling to herself, she went into her room and got ready for bed.

As she climbed beneath the covers, she thought about how nice it was to have everyone here under one roof. Inviting them here was a great idea. It took her no time to fall asleep.

When she woke up the next morning, she heard the murmur of voices downstairs. Hurrying out of bed, she rushed through her morning duties and dressed before going downstairs.

"Well, good morning, sleepyhead," June teased as she held out a cup of coffee.

"I'm so sorry," Stella said. "I didn't mean to sleep in so late."

"Oh, give her a break, Junie," Noah said. "She's on vacation."

"I'm just teasing," June said.

"Thank you," Stella said as she took the coffee from her daughter. "You guys are up earlier than I expected."

"Habit." Will shrugged.

"I guess having everyone under one roof made you sleep better," June said.

Of course she would understand. June was a mother.

"I guess so," Stella said. "So, what do we want to do today?"

"I figured you were eager to take us into town," June said. "I would love to check out some of the stores you told me about."

"Of course!" Stella said. "You're going to love them."

Excited, everyone loaded up in two cars to drive into town. The men went off to explore on their own, leaving the women and kids on their own to shop. They spent the rest of the morning and early afternoon browsing the stores. They ate lunch at the pub and went to Darlene's bakery for dessert. Stella introduced everyone and June oohed and awed over the cases filled with sinful delights.

"You're a baking magician," June crooned after her first bite of one of Darlene's cakes. "I would get so fat living here."

Beaming, Darlene thanked her. When the kids distracted June, Darlene quietly asked, "How's the visit going?"

"Great!"

"Have you …"

Stella gave a quick shake of the head. "Not yet. I'm letting her fall in love with the place first."

"Ah, I see."

"Okay," June said, joining Stella at the counter again. "Darlene, it was lovely to meet you, but I think it's time to get these kids back to the cabin."

"It was a pleasure meeting you as well, June."

With two cranky children in tow, Stella and June left the bakery to go meet up with the guys at the general store. They found them seated at the counter with drinks in front of them as they laughed at something Howie had said.

"Hello!" Howie greeted them. "You must be June."

"That's me," June said in a rush. "Hey, Will, I think we should get these heathens back."

Will sighed, "Well, gentleman, it was fun while it lasted. Duty calls. Thanks, Howie."

"You're welcome. I'll see you guys around."

While her family went to the car, Stella stayed behind to ask Howie, "Do I want to know what was in those glasses?"

"Probably not." He grinned. "It might be a good idea if you and June drive back to the cabin though."

"Got it."

She joined her family and they headed back to the cabin. The kids were so wound up from too much sugar that Stella offered to take them on an afternoon walk. Grateful for a break, June and Will jumped at the idea.

CHAPTER 25

That evening, Caleb came over for dinner. The introductions went smoother than Stella expected. Of course, she had Noah to thank for that. Like his father had been, he was good at handling his sister.

After dinner, while cleaning up, June nudged Stella and whispered, "Noah's right about Caleb. I like him."

Hearing that sent a wave of relief over Stella, and she realized that she had been tense all evening waiting for June to have another one of her snits.

"I'm glad. He's been a great friend."

June glanced over her shoulder at the kids, who were busy playing with Boomer, before turning back to her mother. "He's handsome too."

Cheeks flaming, Stella hissed, "June!"

Shrugging, June said, "Well, he is. Not that I'm encouraging you or anything. I know it's too soon for all of us."

And just like that, Stella's heart fell. Why did June's statement disappoint her so much? She wasn't interested in Caleb that way. Was she?

Remembering the way her body had reacted to him before, she frowned. Feeling extremely hot all of a sudden, she excused herself and went outside onto the porch. She took a deep breath, welcoming the cold sting in her lungs.

June's comment had really sent her head spinning. She didn't want to be attracted to Caleb. She was still very much in love with her husband. *Late* husband, she reminded herself.

The door opened behind her, and June came out to stand beside her. "I'm sorry. I didn't mean to upset you. I shouldn't have said anything."

"It's okay. It just caught me off guard, that's all."

"Yeah. I'm sorry. I'm trying to be supportive."

Stella sighed and wrapped an arm around her daughter's shoulders. "I know you are, and I appreciate it. Just maybe try a little less?"

June chuckled. "Yeah, I think that might be best. The thought of you being with someone else is still too weird for me. Forget I said Caleb is handsome. Let's both strike it from our memory."

"I don't think that's necessary." She kissed June's cheek. "But thank you."

"I *am* trying. This place … makes it easy. I see why you're enjoying your time here."

Here it was. The perfect opening to bring up the vacation home. But Stella was so afraid of ruining the nice day they'd shared.

"What is it?" June asked, turning to face her. "What's wrong?"

"Nothing is wrong. I've just been thinking about something, but I don't want to upset you."

"What is it?"

She figured now was as good a time as any, so Stella said, "Well, I was thinking of coming back here to visit.

The town is lovely, and the people are amazing, and I was thinking about possibly buying a home here—a vacation home that we could all use."

She held her breath and waited for June to process.

Finally, June said, "I think that's a great idea."

"What?"

Smiling now, June said, "I know I've been a pain in the ass about this trip, but I think I'm starting to get it now. The change has been good for all of us, I think. And I see how much you like it here. I do, too. I would love to come back when we can actually swim in that big lake back there."

Stella couldn't believe it. This was too easy. She was still waiting for the catch. Or the tantrum. Because June's whole attitude about this place had done a one-eighty.

"Mom, I said I'm okay with it," June reminded her. "Not that I have any say in what you do with your money or your life. I'm sorry if I made you feel that way."

Staring at her, Stella asked, "Who are you and what have you done with my daughter?"

June groaned. "Have I really been that much of a brat? I mean, I know I haven't made this holiday easy for you, but I hope I haven't been that bad!"

Laughing, Stella said, "Oh, June, I do love you. You know that, right?"

"I love you, too, Mom. But seriously, have I been such a bitch that you were really scared to tell me you're considering buying a house here?"

"Well …"

June scoffed. "I mean, it's not like you're talking about *moving* here. It would just be a vacation home."

Something about that statement didn't sit right with Stella, but she didn't know why, so she remained silent and bit her lip.

"Brrr, it's freezing out here," June said. "Let's head back inside and find something warm to drink."

Together, they went back inside and joined the men, who were playing Rummy.

"After this hand, deal us in," June said.

"How about some Hot Toddies?" Stella suggested. Everyone agreed, so she got started making them. June joined her.

"The kids are having so much fun with Boomer," June told her. "Look at them."

Stella smiled. "I'm not sure who's having more fun, the kids or Boomer."

"Maybe we should rethink the dog thing. They have dog daycares, you know."

"You're kidding."

"Nope."

By the time they were finished preparing the warm beverages, the guys were done with their game and dealing a new one. Caleb had disappeared to the bathroom.

Noah, of course, jumped at the opportunity to discuss the man behind his back. "So, Junie, was I right about Caleb, or are you still afraid he's taking advantage of our vulnerable mother?"

"Excuse me?" Stella sputtered.

"You're a jerk," June said but she was laughing. "Yes, Noah, you were right. He's a great guy."

"Your sudden change of heart doesn't happen to have anything to with the fact that he's C.J. Abrahams, does it?" Will teased.

Swatting his arm playfully, June said, "You're just as bad as Noah! And … maybe."

Everyone laughed. Caleb returned and they focused on the game at hand. Laughter filled every inch of the cabin and the adults drank and playfully badgered one another as they played cards. The kids watched a funny movie, their own laughter mingling with that of their elders. Stella was having so much fun that she hated for the night to end.

But alas, it had to. June and Will said goodnight and corralled the kids up the stairs, while Stella, Caleb, and Noah cleaned up.

"Well, that was a lot more fun than I expected," Noah said. "We should get Junie drunk more often."

"I heard that!" June yelled from upstairs.

"Whoops." Noah feigned regret but the twinkle in his eyes belied his amusement. "Man, Mom, you can make a great Hot Toddy." He rubbed at his eyes. "I should probably head to bed, too. You two behave."

Stella scoffed as Noah got to his feet. "Go on with you."

"Goodnight, Caleb," Noah said before kissing his mother's temple. "Goodnight, Mom."

Watching him weave his way up the stairs, Stella realized she was a little drunker than she'd realized.

"Whoa, are you okay?" Caleb asked as he reached out to steady her. "Should I help you up the stairs?"

Imagining him in her bedroom sent a rush of heat through her. Feeling foolish, she cleared her throat.

"Thank you, but I think I'll be fine. I'll probably sit in front of the fire for a little bit before making my way upstairs."

His lips curved into a lopsided smile. "Want some company, or would you rather be alone?"

She sighed wistfully. "You're probably tired. I'll be okay alone."

"But you're not really alone. Not tonight."

"It's so nice having them here. I didn't realize how much I missed them."

Nodding, he took her by the hand and led her to the sofa. She sat down, while he tended the fire. She watched him in silent appreciation. Her mind wandered as she wondered how different this trip would have been without him.

"There," Caleb said as he stood back up. "Your fire is good. I guess I'll get going."

"Don't," she heard herself say. She wasn't sure who was more surprised, her or Caleb.

His brows dipped into a contemplative frown as his eyes searched her face. Feeling self-conscious, Stella sat up a little straighter.

"Are you sure?" he asked. "You look sleepy."

"Mmm," she murmured and nodded. "I am, but I'm not ready for you to go yet."

His gaze met hers, and her breath hitched in her chest. Heat skittered across her skin, leaving it flushed in its wake. She told herself it was the mixture of the warmth from the fire and the alcohol. Suddenly, her eyes dropped to his mouth, her gaze tracing the outline of his lips. What would they feel like against her own?

That heat left her skin and struck somewhere deep inside her, making her squirm in her seat.

His eyes, the color of soft, worn leather, still held hers. A shiver ran through her, the hairs on her arms standing up along a ripple of gooseflesh.

Caleb swallowed hard, his Adam's apple bobbing slowly in his throat. Her gazed followed the movement and a soft sigh slipped from her as she fought the urge to nuzzle his neck just under his chin.

"Goodnight, Stella." His voice was rough and laden with barely repressed restraint.

Afraid her own voice would give her away, she nodded. Caleb whistled for Boomer, who reluctantly rose from his spot by the fire and followed his master out of the cabin.

When the door closed, Stella let out a small, humiliated cry. Burying her face in her hands, she silently chastised herself for her unforgivable behavior. She was a terrible woman. A horrible excuse for a wife. She'd come here to process her grief over her late husband, and here she was acting like some ... some hussy!

"I'm sorry, Dale," she whispered. "So very sorry."

Feeling wretched, she toppled over on the sofa, pulling the blanket over her so she could hide from the world.

CHAPTER 26

Christmas Eve finally arrived, bringing its typical childlike excitement. Even Stella felt slightly giddy this morning. While the kids were excited about the impending gifts, she couldn't wait to take them into town for the big Christmas celebration. They were going to love it; she just knew it.

"What time does this thing start?" June asked when she sat down at the kitchen table.

"Noon," Stella replied, "But from what I understand, it doesn't really pick up until around three or four. Dinner begins at six."

Watching Stella pull her breakfast casserole from the oven, June said, "I still don't see how downtown can possibly look even more magical than it does. These people really do go all out for the holidays. I thought that only happened on TV."

Grinning, Stella said, "I know, but if it's anything like the Welcome Christmas shindig, then prepare to be even more amazed. I don't know how they do it. Maybe it's elves?"

"Elves?" Noah entered the kitchen and groggily went to the coffee pot. "What about elves?"

"Mom thinks the townspeople get help from them to decorate the town."

Noah grunted. "Interesting."

Rolling her eyes, Stella said, "Just you wait and see."

"You keep saying that," Noah said. "I hope we aren't underwhelmed because you've got us expecting the North Pole experience."

The two women laughed, while Noah helped himself to a serving of casserole. Will joined them and the adults enjoyed a quiet breakfast together before the kids came barreling down the stairs a little while later.

June served the kids breakfast and Stella began to clean up the kitchen. The two men stayed at the table, talking and teasing the children.

Stella smiled as the happy sounds of home surrounded her. When they left, the cabin was going to be awfully quiet. Just thinking about it made her a little sad. She quickly shook off the negative thoughts. There was no time for that today. No, today was going to be a happy day. An exciting day. A *magical* day. At least for the children, if no one else.

"Grandma, when do we get to go to the party?" Logan asked.

"Not until after lunch."

"After you're finished with your breakfast, you need to go upstairs with your dad to finish wrapping gifts," June said. "Grandma and I have to cook for the party and we don't need you underfoot."

Both children nodded.

"I'm going to go get some firewood from the lean-to," Noah said. "I noticed we were low last night."

"Can I help?" Logan asked eagerly.

"Sure, but you have to bundle up."

"Okay!"

The boy took off like a shot, making the adults laugh.

"If only that excitement about helping out with chores wouldn't disappear," Will said.

"You've still got a few years before those pesky teenage years," Stella assured him. "Enjoy it while you can."

"Oh, come on," Noah said. "We weren't that bad, were we?"

Sending him a smile, Stella said, "I wouldn't say you were bad, but like all teenagers, you pitched a fit whenever asked to do anything around the house."

"Hey," June protested. "I always helped."

"Oh, you both helped. But you don't think I heard all that grumbling under your breath and the irritation in each stomp of your feet? Not to mention the way you slammed things down or slammed cabinet doors and drawers."

"I don't remember."

"Of course you don't," Stella chided. "You're not supposed to. It's all part of being a teenager."

Noah and Logan bundled up and headed outside. They made two trips, fully stocking the firewood rack. After that was done, Logan and his sister went upstairs with their dad to finish wrapping presents, and Noah went back outside. He didn't give a reason, and Stella didn't ask. Even though it was cold, she understood the draw of the outdoors here.

She found her thoughts returning to the possibility of purchasing a second home here. It had been days since she'd heard any news of available houses, and she wondered if maybe she should contact Celia to check in.

"Okay," June said, brushing her hands on her apron. "I think I'm going to enjoy another cup of coffee. Would you like one?"

Sliding the two casseroles into the oven, Stella shook her head. "No, thank you. I think I'm going to go upstairs and shower while everyone is busy."

"Okay."

When Stella got to the top of the stairs, she heard the muffled sound of talking and laughter behind the door of the room June shared with her husband. The sound warmed her heart as she went into her own room to shower and change.

When she returned downstairs, she saw that the kids were now watching a Christmas movie on the TV, June and Will were chatting quietly at the table in the kitchen, and Noah was still absent.

"I wonder what Noah is up to out there?" Stella said.

June shrugged. "I think I heard some talking. Maybe he's hanging out with Caleb?"

At the mention of Caleb, awareness zipped through Stella. She hadn't seen him since their awkward moment the other night. Remembering it now, a fresh wave of embarrassment overcame her. Given the way Caleb had rushed out of here only confirmed how inappropriate her behavior had been. Clearly, he wasn't interested in her like that and only wanted to be friends.

Not that she was looking for a relationship right now. Goodness, what *was* she thinking? It was too soon to be considering that, wasn't it? Since just thinking about it made her feel unfaithful, she was sure it was. She wasn't ready, and Caleb obviously wasn't either.

But why? Did he have some secret girlfriend stashed away somewhere? Was he trying to get over an ex? Stella suddenly realized that she had no idea what the man's relationship status was, or if there even was one.

It didn't matter. She wasn't interested anyway, and apparently neither was he.

When she sighed, June looked at her. "What are you thinking about over there?"

"What? Oh, nothing."

"It doesn't look like nothing to me. You look sad. Are you missing Dad?"

Even though it wasn't the complete truth, Stella nodded.

The front door opened just then and Noah walked in with Caleb right behind him. Stella stiffened, immediately standing taller. Just because she was feeling insecure didn't mean Caleb needed to see it.

"Hey, everyone," Caleb said, his voice somehow both smooth, yet gravelly. "Is everyone ready for the big day?"

The kids cheered and Stella tried to ignore the warm hum that was thrumming through her body. Then Caleb's rich, brown eyes found hers and that hum kicked up into a racing pulse.

Oh, dear. This was not good.

Feeling the heat in her cheeks, she pressed her hands to them. It felt wrong to feel such an attraction to a man who wasn't her husband. She hoped her children hadn't noticed.

"Would you like some coffee?" June offered, snapping Stella back to attention.

"Yes, I'll make you some," she said in a rush as she crossed the room. "I've got it June. You sit."

Raising her eyebrows in surprise, June sank back down onto her chair.

"Don't go to any trouble for me," Caleb said. "I'm good. I've had enough already."

"Oh, okay," Stella said, avoiding his gaze. "Then how about some breakfast? Have you eaten? There's some leftover breakfast casserole in the fridge. I can heat some up for you."

"I ate." Caleb's forehead wrinkled in a frown of concern. "Are you feeling okay? You look a little flushed."

Stella froze for a couple of seconds before she waved off his concern with a hand. "That's probably because I just got out of the shower. I'm fine. Excited about today, but absolutely positively fine."

Hearing the panicked insistence in her voice, Stella felt mortified. Even more so when she realized everyone was staring at her. All of the adults, at least. The kids were too engrossed with their movie to notice their grandmother rambling on like a crazy person.

Noah broke through the awkward tension hanging heavily in the air by saying, "I'm going to head into town early with Caleb and help with set up." He looked at his mother. "Unless you need me here for something?"

Stella shook her head.

"Is there a lot to do?" Will asked. "I would be happy to help out also."

Caleb smiled. "Sure, there's plenty to do if you'd like to join us."

The three men left together, leaving Stella and June alone with the kids. June was staring at her mother, so Stella cleared her throat and turned to the oven to check on the status of the casseroles so she wouldn't have to speak. How in the world was she supposed to explain her attraction to Caleb to her daughter, of all people?

"What was that?" June asked.

"Mmm, what was what?" Stella pretended to be more interested in her task than June's question.

"The way you were rambling on like that. It was odd. Did something happen between you two the other night after we all went to bed?"

Stella's breath caught in her throat and then she swallowed hard. "Nothing happened. We chatted a little bit and then he left."

"So, no disagreement or anything like that?"

Forcing a smile, Stella shook her head. "No. Caleb and I are fine. We're friends."

June's head tilted as she scrutinized her mother even more. "Are you sure? Because there's this weird … vibe coming off of you. Like you're nervous or embarrassed or something."

"Honey, I'm fine. I'm just excited about today. The kids are going to have so much fun. And you, too, I hope. Perhaps that's why I might seem a little nervous. I want you to enjoy this holiday. Maybe I'm putting a little too much pressure on myself."

She had to admit, the story sounded good, and it was mostly true.

"Mom, there's no need to put pressure on yourself," June said. "I'm already having a good time and so are the kids. This trip has been everything I didn't know we needed. Thank you."

"Oh, honey," Stella said as her eyes filled with joyful tears. "It makes me so happy to hear that."

"Well, goodness, there's no reason to cry," June said as she rose and came to hug Stella tightly. "I love you, Mom."

"I love you, too, June. So much. I'm so glad you're having a good time. I'm so glad you guys came. It was silly of me to think I needed to be away from you all at Christmas."

"Yeah, well, I tried to tell you," June teased. "Why do you think I gave you such a hard time? The whole idea of being apart at Christmas was absurd."

"Maybe, but it led us here, which has been wonderful."

June nodded. "I agree. I guess things really do happen for a reason, huh?"

"Sometimes."

"Now, let's go sit with the kids until it's time for lunch. Then we'll be off to your winter wonderland Christmas celebration."

Linking her arm through her daughter's, Stella let June lead her into the living room.

CHAPTER 27

After lunch, the two women loaded the kids in the car and drove into town. As they neared downtown, the kids' eyes went wide at the sight of all the lights and decorations hanging form the trees, light poles, and building eaves. They scrambled out of the car so fast that both Stella and June simultaneously told them not to take off.

Groaning in protest, the kids reluctantly held back and stayed close. June sent a text to Will, who told her he and Noah were in the picnic area by the big tree.

"Wow," June said as they headed for the tree. "You weren't kidding. Look at this place. I thought it was already decorated over-the-top. This is amazing."

Lights dripped along the buildings and dangled across the road between the light poles. Every bush and tree was illuminated. The store windows were still painted with wintry snowscapes and colorful Christmas scenes.

Fake snow filled the potted plants, spilling over onto the real snow-covered ground around them. Ribbon curls hung from the trees and the lamp posts were wound with thick red and white ribbon. Christmas music filled the air, as did the welcoming smells of sugar, cinnamon, and savory spices from the buffet tables.

Stella stopped by one of the buffet tables to drop off their casseroles before they continued on to the tree.

"Look! Look! Mom, look!"

"Wow! Look, Mom!"

The kids gawked at the enormous tree in the center of the square even though they'd already seen it on their previous trip to town.

"I see it," June said, sounding pretty awed herself. "Mom, this is just …"

"I know," Stella said, grinning. "It gets more beautiful every time you see it, doesn't it?"

"There you are!" Noah smiled as he and Will joined them.

"Honey, isn't this place great?" Will asked his wife.

Nodding, June replied, "It is."

Will looked down at the kids. "Who wants fudge? Or candied apples?"

"I want it all!" Logan exclaimed, making them all laugh.

"Let's go," Will said, taking June's hand.

"Go," Stella said. "Have fun. I'm going to go say hello to Darlene."

Noah stayed behind with Stella. "So, have you heard about any new real estate listings?"

"No, I haven't. I don't think anything is going to be available until spring anyway. The market for lake homes isn't too hot in the middle of winter, especially around Christmas."

"You're probably right."

They found Darlene at the dessert table. The women hugged one another in greeting. Stella offered to help but Darlene told her there was nothing to really do.

"Merry Christmas Eve," Howie said as he and Caleb walked up to them.

"Merry Christmas Eve," Stella said, giving him a hug. "Are you closing the store for the day?"

"Nah. People might need some last-minute things. I have one of the teenagers manning the register right now."

"That's nice of you."

"Where are the kids?" Caleb asked.

"Off getting treats."

"Ah, good for them." Howie said.

"Well, I need to check in at the bakery," Darlene said. "I've got pies in the oven for later."

Stella gave an appreciative groan. "I can't wait." Then she realized that Caleb was alone. "Where's Boomer? Doesn't he get to partake in the festivities?"

Caleb laughed. "No, he's home. Trust me, it's for the best tonight."

"Poor guy."

"Oh, no. He will get plenty of treats tomorrow."

Howie's phone beeped. "It looks like I'm needed at the store. You kids have fun."

"Need any help?" Caleb asked.

"Nah, I got it."

He walked away, leaving Stella and Caleb alone. Chewing her lower lip, Stella looked everywhere but at him as the tension between them grew awkward.

Did he feel it too, or was she making a big deal out of nothing? What was wrong with her? He was still her friend, and it's not like she'd made a pass at him or anything.

"Hey," Caleb said softly, placing a hand on her arm. "Are you okay? You've been acting strange lately."

"I'm fine."

"Are you sure? Have I done something wrong?"

She shook her head. "Not at all."

Nope. The tension between them was all her fault.

Even though his expression told her he didn't completely believe her, he nodded. "How about we go find your family?"

Before she could respond, he took her gloved hand in his and guided her towards the food carts. The action was so natural, yet intimate, it took her breath away. Telling herself she was being silly, she forced her lungs back into action and begged her now racing heart to calm down.

They spotted her family sitting at a picnic bench enjoying their treats but when Stella started in their direction, she felt a gentle tug on her hand.

"Let me buy you a treat," Caleb said, nodded at the food carts. "What's your pleasure? Cotton candy? Candied apples? Roasted chestnuts? Funnel cake?"

"Oh, my. I couldn't tell you the last time I had a funnel cake."

"Funnel cake it is," he said, pulling her to the cart.

"How is funnel cake Christmassy?"

Someone walked buy with their newly purchased funnel cake and she saw how. In addition to powdered sugar, the cake had red and green sugar crystals sprinkled on top of them.

Caleb ordered one cake and two hot chocolates to go with it. When he handed her the funnel cake, she saw that there were also tiny snowflakes sprinkled on top.

They joined her family, sitting beside each other to share the dessert. Stella couldn't help herself and moaned in pleasure with each bite she took.

"Have you guys visited the reindeer food booth yet?" Caleb asked the kids.

"The what?" Logan asked with sticky red lips from his candied apple.

"Oh, man," Caleb said. "It's really neat. You follow the recipe card and scoop the ingredients for reindeer food into your bag to take home. Then tonight, you sprinkle it outside for Santa's reindeer to munch on while he's putting your gifts under the tree."

"Really?" Lizzie said, turning to her parents. "Please, please, please, can we do it?"

Chuckling, Will said, "Of course we can."

"Just when I think this place can't get any more festive," June said.

"Oh, wait until the after dinner caroling," Caleb said. "The whole town joins in."

June's mouth fell open, then she caught herself and said, "You're kidding. Well, I guess I stand corrected." She looked at Stella. "Mom, you were right about this place. It's simply magical. Thank you for inviting us."

"You're welcome." Stella took a sip of her hot chocolate, while she blinked back tears.

Caleb gave her gentle nudge and whispered, "Merry Christmas, Stella."

At a loss for words, she nodded. It was a merry Christmas, indeed. She was so glad she'd found this place.

June and the kids raced off to the reindeer food stand, and Noah and Will wandered off in search of some holiday spirits. Stella and Caleb finished off their funnel cake and then wandered around taking in all the booths and the excitement in the air.

"So, it looks like you've gotten everything you wanted this Christmas," Caleb said. "Are you happy?"

"I did and I am. I was so worried about June, but your little town has somehow managed to work its magic on her."

"It's always weird hearing people say that. To me, this place is just home, and this," he paused to gesture around them, "is normal."

"It's enchanting. Magical."

"If you say so." He draped an arm around her shoulders as they walked.

She wasn't sure if he even realized what he was doing, but she wasn't about to ruin the moment. Instead, she nestled closer to his side, letting her head fall against his shoulder.

CHAPTER 28

When dinner time arrived, everyone lined up at the buffet tables to wait their turn. Everyone took their time, chatting as they slowly moved along. Then they spread out everywhere to eat. Then it was time to tackle the dessert tables.

After dinner, everyone gathered in the square around the tree to sing. Once the caroling was over, people stood around chatting, while others began to drift away to collect their dishes and head home.

Logan and Lizzie couldn't stop yawning, so June and Will took them home, leaving Noah and Stella behind.

"Well done, Mom," Noah said. "This whole day has been incredible. The town is amazing. The people are amazing."

"I'm glad you think so."

"I don't think June missed our family dinner tonight at all."

"I think you're right. She seemed happy."

Noah nodded. "Happier than I've seen her in a while." He gently elbowed her. "So, you and Caleb seem to be getting along well."

Her heart skipped. "Why wouldn't we be getting along?"

He shrugged a shoulder. "Things were weird the other day, so I thought maybe you guys had a fight or something."

She shook her head but didn't elaborate.

"He's a great guy," Noah continued. "It would be a shame to lose a friend like him."

She stopped walking and turned to look at him. "What are you trying to say, Noah?"

"That I approve."

She frowned. "Since when do I need your approval to have friends?"

"You don't, of course, but when I see my mother walking hand in hand with someone, I feel compelled to weigh in, especially when I know how much you worry about your children's feelings."

"You saw that?"

Noah laughed quietly. "Mom, I think the whole town saw it. It's not like you were trying to hide it."

Feeling the color drain from her face, Stella gasped. "Did June see? Oh, God. She's probably mad at me."

"No, Mom, she's not."

"She's not? How do you know? Did she say something?"

"She did. She told me that you two look good together. She also told me she liked seeing you so happy. We both do."

Feeling relieved, Stella blew out a breath. "You don't think it's too soon?"

"Mom, it's been *two years*. Dad wouldn't want you to be lonely, and for what it's worth, I think he would like Caleb."

She couldn't believe she was having this conversation with her son. However, she was also glad it was happening. Even though she'd said otherwise, she *did* need her children's approval to move on. Maybe approval wasn't the right word. More like blessing. Yes, that was what she needed. Their blessing. The last thing she wanted to do was make them feel like she was trying to replace Dale. That could never happen.

But her heart told her that Noah was right; Dale wouldn't want her to be alone for the rest of her life.

"Do you really think Caleb is interested in me?" she asked. "I mean, what if he just wants to be friends?"

Noah sent her an incredulous look. "Are you kidding? Have you not seen the way he looks at you? Were you not there today when he held your hand and *shared* a dessert with you?"

"Well, yes, but I was also there the several times he couldn't run out of the cabin fast enough to get away from me."

Noah rolled his eyes. "If you're talking about the other night, *of course* he left. You were drunk, Mom. He's not going to take advantage of you like that. That's not the kind of guy Caleb is." His brows dipped together in a frown. "Were you drinking the other times?"

"Well, yes."

"There you go."

Was that it? She thought back to the times things had gotten weird between them, and if she wasn't mistaken, she'd had quite a bit to drink each time.

They arrived back at the car, and Stella offered to drive since she knew that Noah had indulged in a few drinks. She took them back to the cabin, where it was surprisingly quiet. Then Stella noticed that the drapes were open.

"I think they're out back," she told Noah, as she went to the door.

She saw June and Will sitting on the deck together in a single lounge chair. June was cradled in Will's arms with her back against his chest. They had the big fluffy throw from the sofa covering them. She held a glass of wine, and he had a glass of what Stella assumed was whisky.

"Yeah, I'm not interrupting that," Noah said over Stella's shoulder. "I'll just call it a night. Goodnight, Mom."

He kissed her cheek and disappeared up the stairs. Since she wasn't tired enough to fall asleep yet, Stella poured herself a glass of wine and went to sit in front of the fire for a little bit. She found her tablet and brought up her reading app.

Thirty minutes later, the sliding glass door opened and June and Will stumbled inside. The second June spotted her mother, her already pink cheeks darkened.

"Hey, Mom. We didn't realize you were still up. We heard you and Noah come home and figured you went to bed when you didn't come outside."

"I didn't want to intrude. I thought you guys could use some alone time."

"Thanks," June said as her husband kissed her cheek.

Then he looked at Stella. "Thank you for today. It was a lot of fun. Goodnight."

As he started up the stairs, Stella told him, "You're welcome. Goodnight." She looked back at June, who was sitting down next to her. "So, you two seem happy."

"We really are," June said wistfully. "Everything was wonderful today, from the treats to the food to the people ... I see why you love this place so much."

"Yeah. I think the kids enjoyed themselves."

"Oh, they definitely did. They talked nonstop on the way back to the cabin. They want to come back next year."

"They do?"

June nodded. "Yes, they do. So, Will and I were talking about it, and we were thinking that maybe we should make this our new tradition."

Stella gasped. "Really?"

"Yes, really. I mean, you're talking about buying a house here anyway, right? And we all had so much fun today."

Oh, she recognized that starry eyed look. Leaving June and Will alone on the porch had definitely been the right call.

"Okay then. I guess it's settled. As soon as I find a place, I'll put in an offer."

Grinning widely, June hugged her. "I love you, Mom. Merry Christmas."

"I love you, too, sweetheart. Merry Christmas."

June went up to bed, leaving Stella alone. She got her coat and went out onto the back porch to look out over the water. Sighing contentedly, she took a deep breath, slowly inhaling in the crisp, cold air.

The sound of snuffling drew her attention to the cabin next door. As expected, Boomer came hurdling across the yard. Unexpectedly, a small shadow followed him.

"Hey, there, buddy," Stella said, kneeling down to pet him. "Oh, my goodness! Who is your friend?" She scooped up the wiggling puppy who immediately began licking her face. "Aren't you the cutest little thing!"

Caleb came rushing up. Clearly flustered, he raked a hand through his hair. "I didn't expect to see you out here this late," he said.

"Everyone else is in bed but I wasn't ready to call it a night just yet. I see you got Boomer a friend."

"She's not mine; she's a Christmas present. I'm just holding her until tomorrow."

"Oh, well, someone is going to be very happy tomorrow. She's adorable."

"You think?"

"Oh, yes. In fact, she's so adorable that I might steal her and keep her for myself." She looked into the pup's caramel-colored eyes. "What do you think? I bet you would love to stay here with me, wouldn't you?"

The puppy responded with an excited yip and began licking her chin again.

"She does like you," Caleb said as he gave the pup a rub.

Stella bent down and set the pup on the porch. She immediately ran after Boomer, who was sniffing around the yard.

"So, did everyone have fun today?" Caleb asked.

"Yes. So much that they want to come back next year."

"Seriously?"

"Yes! Can you believe it? They want to make it our new Christmas tradition. They're all on board with me buying a house here, too. I can't believe it. I mean, I knew they would have a great time, but I wasn't expecting this."

She realized Caleb was quiet. When she looked at him, she saw that he was looking out at the water. Her excitement waned, and she wasn't sure what to think. She'd expected him to be happy about learning she was coming back.

"That's great news," he finally said.

"Yeah," she said, still confused by his lackluster reaction. After her earlier conversation with Noah, she'd expected him to be at least a little bit excited about the news of her buying a house here. "Well, I guess I should call it a night. The kids will have us up early tomorrow."

She turned away from him, but he grabbed her arm. "Stella, wait."

"What?" The question came out a little gruffer than intended.

"I had a good time today," he said, his voice low and huskier than usual, sending a shiver along her skin. "And I'm glad that you're planning to buy a house here."

She could sense there was more, so she said, "But?"

He swallowed hard and moved closer to her. Having to look up to see him now, she drew in an expectant breath as she tilted her head back.

"No buts, just this."

His mouth came down to meet hers, sending a jolt of heat through her. His lips started out gentle, slowly increasing in pressure and finally moving against hers. Her lips parted, and their tongues met. A low moan vibrated through them both; she couldn't tell which one of them it originated from. He tasted like whisky, the hints of smoky nuttiness dancing along her tongue and mixing with dark cherry of the wine lingering on her own tongue.

His hands tangled in her hair, cupping her face and holding her in place while he plundered and explored her mouth. She drew her arms up to link her hands behind his neck as she pressed herself against him.

With a groan, he pulled back to rest his forehead against hers. His eyes locked with hers and she felt the tug of desire at her core.

Chest heaving, he whispered, "You've been drinking."

"So have you."

His eyes searched hers and she noticed there were streaks of gold mixed with the brown of his irises. "Is this okay? I mean, you're not too drunk?"

"No," she whispered. "I only had one glass of wine. Are you?"

"No."

"Okay."

"Okay."

They continued to stand there staring into one another's eyes until Boomer gave a low whine. Stella wasn't sure how much time had passed but she did realize that she was slightly chilled. When she shivered, Caleb ran his hands up and down her arms to warm her.

"You're cold," Caleb said. "You should go inside."

"I'm good," she said, giving him a hint of a smile. "I'm really good actually."

He smiled. "Even so. You have a house full of guests and tomorrow is Christmas. I'll come by in the morning before I head out to my dad's."

And then he was kissing her again. She put her arms around him, drawing him against her. He growled deep in his chest before finally stepping away from her.

"Good grief, woman, you might just kill me."

She laughed. "What does that mean?"

His eyes locked on hers again. This time, they were full of fire and need. "It means that I want you so badly right now that I'm having a hard time reminding myself that I'm a gentleman. What I really want to do is take you inside and make you scream my name so loud that it echoes across the lake."

Oh. My. God.

Her knees actually wobbled.

"Whoa. Easy there. If I have to carry you inside, I'm not going to be able to leave."

She swallowed; her tongue now glued to the roof of her mouth. Mouth too dry to speak, she nodded. He leaned forward to brush his lips across her forehead.

"Good night, Stella. Merry Christmas." He whistled for the dogs as he strode back across the yard to his house.

Staring after him, Stella wrapped her arms around her middle. Well, how about that.

Feeling giddy, she turned and went back inside. Although she wasn't sure sleep would come easy tonight. Not after he'd gotten her all worked up. And wasn't that a great thing?

CHAPTER 29

Christmas morning arrived with fervent energy. The kids woke everyone up before the sun began to peek over the horizon. Stella dutifully went straight to the kitchen to get coffee going and to warm some leftover breakfast casserole in the oven.

Once the adults had their cups of caffeine in hand, everyone gathered around the tree to watch the kids tear into their gifts. After they were done, the adults exchanged their gifts. Then they moved into the kitchen for breakfast.

"Guys, I need you to clean up your mess before you do anything else," June told the kids.

Groaning in protest, they grabbed a trash bag and got busy picking up ripped up paper, bows, and ribbons from the floor. Will gathered the bags and went to take them outside. When he opened the door, Boomer ran inside.

"Merry Christmas," Will said as Caleb came inside.

The kids took one look at the puppy in Caleb's arms and began squealing in excitement. The poor pup tried clawing her way up his chest and over his shoulder.

"Shhh!" June hissed. "You're scaring the poor little thing to death. Calm down."

The squealing stopped immediately, and the kids ran up to Caleb to pet the puppy. He cautioned them to be easy as he knelt down so they could better reach the squirming pup.

"What's its name?" Lizzie asked.

"I don't know yet," Caleb explained. "She's not mine; she's a gift."

"For us?" Logan asked, his voice hopeful.

"Sorry, but no."

Both kids deflated with simultaneous 'awws'.

"Caleb, would you like coffee?" Stella asked.

"Sure, but first you need to take your gift."

Her gift? She frowned. She wasn't expecting anything from him, but she was secretly glad she'd bought him a little something. It was just a sweater, but at least she had something to give him in return.

She walked over to him and took the puppy from him so he could get her gift. "Hello, little angel," she cooed. "You've created quite the stir this morning."

"Merry Christmas, Stella," Caleb said.

Nuzzling the pup, she replied, "Merry Christmas."

Amusement danced in Caleb's eyes as he nodded at the wriggling bundle of fur in her arms. "Angel sounds like the perfect name for her."

"Yes, well, I think that's up to her new owner, don't you?"

June appeared at her side and whispered in her ear, "I think that's you, Mom."

Understanding dawned on Stella then and she gasped. "What? She's mine? Caleb, you didn't!" She held the puppy up so she touch noses with her. "Are

177

you mine? Oh, you sweet, adorable, little angel. Yes! Angel it is."

Laughter rippled around her as Stella looked at Caleb through a sheen of tears. "I can't believe you did this. How in the world were you able to keep such a secret? Thank you."

She rushed to hug him, careful to keep from squishing the puppy between them.

"You're welcome. I'm glad you like her."

"Like her? I *love* her!"

He kissed her forehead and said, "I'm glad. I thought the gig was up last night when you surprised us outside."

"Are you kidding?" Noah asked. "After everything we went through to keep her a secret?"

Stella spun around to face her son. "You knew?"

"Of course I knew! Caleb asked me if I thought it was a good idea, and I helped pick her out. I can't believe you almost ruined the surprise."

Stella set Angel down so the kids could play with her, while Caleb told everyone how he'd taken the dogs out for a potty break last night and Stella had been on the back porch. Although he left out the best part of the story, Stella's body warmed at the memory of their kiss.

And now he'd given her a puppy. Could the man be any more perfect?

"Oh!" she exclaimed. "Your gift. Hey, Logan, grab Caleb's gift from under the tree please."

The boy retrieved the box and brought it over to them. Caleb opened it and thanked her.

"I know it's not much," Stella started and Caleb cut her off, saying, "It's perfect. You can never have enough sweaters around here. Thank you."

"You're welcome," she said with a smile.

"Well, I hate to do this, but I need to get to my dad's."

"I'll walk you out," Stella said.

She put on her coat and followed him out onto the front porch. She'd barely closed the door before he pulled her into his arms and kissed her, long and slow.

When they broke apart, he whispered, "Merry Christmas, Stella. I hope you have a great rest of your day."

"You, too. I imagine we'll all be napping this afternoon."

His eyes darkened. "I wish I could join you."

Heat flooded her, turning her face crimson at the thought of 'napping' with him.

"You're cute when you blush," he said.

"Oh, stop," she said.

"I have to go," he said hoarsely.

"Go. Tell your family I said Merry Christmas."

He gave her quick kiss this time and then turned and clopped down the stairs. She hugged herself as she watched him go. She couldn't believe he'd given her a puppy. She also couldn't believe they were doing whatever you called it these days. Making out? Dating? Going steady? She didn't even know the proper term for it.

But she did know that she was enjoying it.

When she went inside, Noah said, "You're looking a little flushed there, Mom. Are you feeling okay?"

"Hush, Noah," she chided.

Noah chuckled, and June grabbed her own coat before silently slipping out the back door. Stella looked between Noah and Will and sighed.

Oh, boy. It looked like June wasn't as okay with her and Caleb as she wanted everyone to think.

Without saying anything, Stella crossed the cabin and followed June outside. Her daughter was standing on the shore of the lake. Stella cautiously walked down to join her. When she stopped to stand beside June, the younger woman sighed.

"I'm sorry," June said. "It's a little harder than I thought it would be, seeing you with a man who isn't dad. I mean, I want you to be happy. I do. It's just … strange."

"It's strange for me too," Stella admitted.

June turned to her. "I *am* happy for you. Caleb is a great guy."

"But he's not your dad."

June nodded.

Stella wrapped an arm around her and said, "It's okay to feel that way. I still do."

"You do?"

"Of course. I'm still trying not to feel guilty. Like I'm somehow betraying your father, even though I know I'm not."

"He would want you to be happy."

"I think so, too."

June hugged her tightly. "I'm happy that you're happy. I can't believe he bought you a puppy."

Laughing, Stella said, "I can't believe it either."

"Let's get back inside. It's freezing out here."

Arm in arm, the two women went back inside to join their family.

CHAPTER 30

Puppies were a lot of work. It was like having a new baby in the house. Lucky for Stella, she had plenty of people to help keep track of the rambunctious Angel. But that was going to change tomorrow when everyone went home. She was equal parts excited and sad about having the cabin to herself again.

She grew even sadder when she realized that her time here was almost up as well. The thought of going back to Massachusetts was surreal. Even though she'd been here a short time, Evergreen Point had begun to feel like home, and she was having a hard time imagining being back in the house she used to share with Dale.

Angel gave a little bark, as if saying Stella wouldn't be completely alone now.

Smiling, Stella looked down at the small chocolate Lab. "Don't worry. I haven't forgotten about you."

She scooped her up and nuzzled her as she took her outside to do her business. Everyone else was napping upstairs after the eventful morning. Stella had stayed up to put the ham in the oven.

Once Angel was done, Stella was planning on resting herself as well. She was hoping that little Angel would curl up with her on the sofa for a quick nap.

Seeing that Angel was finished, Stella scooped it up with one of the little bags that Noah had included in his puppy care basket that he gave her for Christmas. She disposed of it in the trash can and then called Angel as she headed back inside. She washed her hands and then settled onto the sofa with Angel for a nap. The small pup obliged, curling up by her legs.

About forty minutes later, the sound of trampling footsteps on the stairs woke Stella.

"I told you to be quiet," June chastised the kids.

"It's fine," Stella said. "I didn't want to sleep too long anyway."

The kids immediately went to Angel, who jumped down on the floor ready to play. Stella suggested they take her outside before she had an accident. The kids eagerly complied.

"They're really enjoying your Christmas present," June said. "They are going to be sad when we leave tomorrow."

"Well, they're more than welcome to come visit her anytime," Stella said. "I'm going to be sad for you guys to leave tomorrow too."

"Me, too, but I guess we need to get back to reality sometime."

Stella grew quiet as her thoughts went back to going home. She was just getting to know Caleb and now she was going to have to leave. What did that mean for them?

"Uh oh," June said. "What's with that face? You're thinking about leaving Caleb, aren't you?"

"Yes. This thing between us is just getting started." Stella sighed heavily. "Once I get back to Massachusetts, I'm sure he'll forget all about me."

"Oh, Mom, I'm sure that's not true." June frowned. "I guess you guys have a lot to talk about, huh?"

"I guess so. I don't see how this can work."

"I'm sure you guys can figure it out. His job is flexible and you don't have a job tying you down. It should be easy enough to travel back and forth, especially if you get a house here."

"What if he doesn't want to be bothered with all that traveling?" Panic edged into Stella's voice. "What if he doesn't want to come to Massachusetts at all?"

"Hey," June walked over and took her hands in hers. "There's no reason to get yourself all worked up, especially not before you talk with Caleb."

"You're right."

June smiled. "You two will figure it all out. I'm sure of it. Why don't you invite him over for dessert tonight? We'll give you guys some privacy to talk."

Stella shook her head. "No. This isn't a conversation we need to have while you guys are here. It can wait. Besides, I want to make the best of your last night here."

"Okay, if that's what you want."

"He's having dinner and stuff with his family anyway."

The door opened and the kids blew back inside with Angel happily leading the way.

"Watch out!" Noah said as he descended the stairs. "Tornado of fun alert!"

Everyone laughed as he made a whooping siren sound. He went into the living area and dropped to all fours as Angel barked and began licking his face, while his niece and nephew climbed on his back.

Stella laughed as she watched them wrestle and play. Then she and June began preparing dinner. Throughout dinner, Stella tried not to think about their time here coming to an end. She couldn't believe it was already time for her family to leave, with her own departure not too far behind.

"Grandma," Logan said. "Thank you for having us here. It was fun. Can we come back again?"

Smiling, Stella replied, "I'm glad you enjoyed yourself. I don't see why we couldn't come back again. We'll have to see."

"Can we come back when we can swim?" Lizzie asked. "I think it would be even more fun in the summer."

"Well, I don't know about this summer. I'm pretty sure these houses are rented out well in advance. I'll have to look into it."

June's eyes met hers, silently thanking her for not mentioning that she was thinking about buying a house here. Stella smiled. Of course, she knew better than to mention the possibility of something that exciting happening. One, because the kids would be extremely disappointed if it didn't happen, and two, because they would relentlessly bug their parents about it every day.

When they were cleaning up, a knock sounded at the door. Noah opened it and then turned to Stella. "Mom, it's for you."

"Go ahead," June said, making a shooing motion. "Go. We'll finish up here, won't we, Noah?"

Seeing his sister's pointed look, Noah quickly agreed. "Sure thing!"

Grateful for the break, Stella snatched her coat from the rack and went out onto the porch to meet Caleb.

"Hi," she said. "I wasn't expecting to see you tonight. How was dinner with your family?"

"It was good. Thanks. I know your family is leaving in the morning, but I was wondering if I could steal you away for a little bit?"

"Oh?" Panic tickled the base of her spine. "Is everything okay?"

"Oh, everything is fine. I just … wanted to see you. If that's okay?"

"Um, yeah. I mean, yes, of course."

He took her hand and led her across the yard to his house. They went inside, took off their coats, and he led the way to the kitchen. Her heart did a somersault when she saw the table set, complete with candles.

"What is this?" she asked.

"I wanted to have dessert with you," he said, pulling out the chair for her to sit.

"This is lovely. Thank you."

Although she was full from dinner, the sight of one of Darlene's pies made her mouth water. Caleb poured them both wine and then sat across from her. She watched as he sliced the pie and expertly slid pieces onto their plates.

She took a bit of the apple pie, her eyes falling shut as she gave a low moan of appreciation. "So good."

"I know. I don't know how she does it."

"She's a treasure; that's for sure." She took a sip of wine, recognizing it as her favorite immediately. "Oh."

"I pay attention," he said. Then he turned sheepish and rolled his eyes. "Okay, maybe Dad helped me out."

She laughed.

"So, I know everyone leaves tomorrow, and you're scheduled to leave in a couple of days."

"Yes." Unease crept under her skin.

"As much as I don't want you to go, I understand you need to get back to your life."

"You don't want me to go?"

"No. What I want is to tie you to my bed upstairs so you never ever leave." He paused when she gasped softly. "But I know that's not practical. I wanted to let you know that you don't have to go *if* you don't want to. I spoke with the Anderson's, and they said they're willing to extend your rental agreement if you'd like."

Her heart jumped at the thought. "Caleb."

"Or you could stay here. In the guest room, of course." He wiggled his eyebrows. "Wouldn't want to scandalize the town."

She chuckled and shook her head. "I don't know. I feel like I should get back to my real life. This whole vacation has been wonderful, but it's just that. A vacation. I can't run from my life forever."

Disappointment flooded his eyes. "What about us? We're just getting started. At least, I thought we were."

"We are," she said quickly. "But it's just …"

"It's just what?"

She set her fork down. "I … I'll have to think about it."

His lips twitched as he searched her face. "Okay."

"We still have a couple of days."

He nodded. "True."

"After that we'll … figure it out."

"I guess it's a good thing I can work anywhere."

"You would come to Massachusetts?"

His brows dipped in confusion. "Of course. Why wouldn't I? Do you not want me to?"

"Oh, no! I do!" She licked her lips. "I really do."

But she would be lying if she said she wasn't nervous. What if he got there and decided he didn't fit in there? What if he hated it? He was so used to the solitude of this place.

"Stella?"

She jumped in surprise. "Yeah?"

"Stop thinking so much. It will work out."

"Will it?"

What if her friends thought she was moving too fast? What if they didn't like him?

"Stella."

"Yeah?"

"Take a deep breath and a sip of wine. There's no reason to jump to the worst conclusion. At least give us a chance."

She nodded. "You're right. I'm sorry."

He reached over and squeezed her hand. Awareness hummed up her arm and settled low in her belly. Color warmed her cheeks, spreading down her neck. Caleb's thumb gently caressed the knuckle of her own thumb.

"I guess I should let you get back to your family."

Her eyes darted up to his. "I suppose that would be the proper thing to do."

Her emotions were a tangled mess. Part of her was grateful that he wasn't pushing the physical side of their relationship, but another part of her couldn't help but feel the burn of rejection. Was he not attracted to her after all? She took a deep, calming breath and reminded herself that he was trying to be respectful of her family.

Besides, she shouldn't even be thinking about sex with him yet, should she? She wasn't even sure what the proper time frame was to wait after the death of your spouse before you got physical with someone else.

"Stella."

Caleb's voice drew her from her pit of doubt. "I'm sorry. My mind keeps drifting."

"To your husband?"

She nodded. "I-I don't know how to do this. If it's even proper."

"Stella, if you aren't ready—"

"It's not that. I don't think ... Goodness, this is embarrassing. I'm sorry. I just don't know what I'm doing. It's been so long and yet somehow, not long enough. Does that make sense? Oh, it probably doesn't."

She buried her face in her hands, and he gently pulled them away to hold them in his own.

"Take a breath, Stella."

She pressed her lips together. "I'm sorry."

"Honey, you don't need to apologize."

Her heart skipped. "Okay."

A slow, wide smile spread across his face and as she absorbed his handsomeness, her anxiety calmed. The laugh lines etched into his face added to his rugged good looks, as did the strands of gray streaking through his chestnut hair, making him look dignified. Add in the warm brown eyes that reminded her of melted caramel, and she felt like a lustful teenager all over again. It bordered on disgraceful.

"Come on," he said. "Let's get you home."

"O-okay."

He walked her back to the cabin and said goodnight. They shared another kiss. Sweet and full of promise. Then she went inside.

"Well, well," Noah teased. "I was beginning to think I was going to have to come over there and drag you home, young lady."

She laughed at the absurdity of his words. "I'm your mother, you know."

"Oh, I know. That's why I feel the need to protect your virtue."

Stella snorted. "Stop."

Noah's grin dimmed. "You know I'm just teasing you, right? I'm happy for you."

She nodded. "Is everyone else asleep?"

"June put the kids down and she and Will are packing now. She already recruited me to help haul some of their Christmas presents home."

"Of course she did." Stella shook her head. "That's our June."

The sound of footsteps signaled the return of June and Will. The four of them gathered around the fire for their final evening together in the cabin.

CHAPTER 31

The next morning went by way too fast, and before Stella knew it, her family was on their way home and she was alone. When she went inside, she looked around the cabin and sighed. While everyone had enjoyed the Christmas decorations, she wasn't looking forward to taking them down, especially since she didn't usually pack up her Christmas stuff at home until after the New Year.

But she wasn't going to be here for the New Year. The thought was jolting. She was going to be home in just a few days. Turning slowly, she bit her lip as tears stung her eyes.

"This is silly," she said to Angel, who was gnawing happily on a chew toy. "I should be happy about going home. As much as I love this cabin, it isn't mine. It isn't home."

Angel stopped chewing and thumped her tail.

"I know you have no idea what I'm saying."

Last night Caleb had suggested she extend her vacation. She'd dismissed the idea almost immediately, but now she found herself considering it. She couldn't possibly do that, could she? What good would come of avoiding going home? She couldn't stay here forever. She had to get back to her life at some point.

The only problem was that the life she was going back to wasn't the life she remembered. At least not the happy one she once had. Dale was gone and would still be gone when she got home. At least here, she wasn't haunted by the memories of him every time she turned around. No, this place felt like hers, and hers alone. Well, not exactly, but close enough.

Guilt overwhelmed her, nearly sending her to her knees. What kind of person was she for wanting to get away from the constant reminders of her late husband? What kind of a wife did that?

Tears spilled down her cheeks. It wasn't that she didn't want to remember Dale and the life she had with him. She absolutely did. She could never forget him, even if she wanted to, but she also needed to move on and learn to live without him. Wasn't that what she was doing here?

Was that it? Being here had helped her with her grief and now, going back felt like she was going backwards instead of forward. Logically, she knew that no one could take the progress she'd made away from her, but it *felt* like it. And that scared her. She didn't want to fall back into that same pattern of despair.

Angel stood and shook herself so hard that she fell over.

Laughing softly, Stella wiped her cheeks. "I suppose you want to go outside again."

She got her coat and took the pup outside. Angel ran down the steps out into the yard, where she squatted.

"Good girl," Stella told her.

She wasn't going to be alone, she reminded herself as she looked at the little chocolate Lab. She had Angel now. The pup would breathe new life and energy into her old house, just as she'd done here.

Angel gave an excited bark seconds before Boomer trotted up to her and gave her a lick. Then he turned and ran to Stella, who dropped into a crouch to greet him.

"Hey, there," she said, petting him.

Caleb wasn't too far behind the dog and came to stand beside her. As she rose, he asked if everyone had gotten off okay. She told him they had.

"Missing them already?" he asked.

"How can you tell?"

"You've been crying."

"Oh, that." Stella wiped her eyes again. "I was thinking about having to go home."

"I take it you haven't given any more thought to staying on for a while."

"I have, but I think it's better if I suck it up and go back. I can't avoid it forever."

"That is true." He rubbed at the whiskers along his jaw. "I guess it would be better to get it over with. Is this the first trip since he's been gone then?"

She nodded. "Yeah. It'll be the first time returning without him."

"I bet that will be hard." He shifted his weight before asking, "Have you thought about moving? You know, downsizing and starting anew?"

Startled, she shook her head. "I don't think the kids are ready for that."

"So, we're back to worrying more about their needs than your own? I thought you'd moved past that by coming here."

Even though she knew he didn't mean to be confrontational, she couldn't help but feel affronted. Clenching her jaw, she crossed her arms and took a step away from him.

"Hey, I didn't mean that how it sounded," Caleb said. "Hell, maybe I did. It frustrates me how you're so quick to ignore your own needs for those of others."

"They're my children. It's my job to put their needs before my own. If you had kids, you'd understand that."

The words came out harsher than she'd intended, and she felt bad for it, especially when she saw the pain that flashed in his eyes.

"I'm sorry," she said. "I didn't mean that."

"No," he said gruffly. "You're right. Boomer, come."

"Caleb, wait. You don't have to leave."

"Yes, I do, because if I stay, we both might say more things that we'll feel sorry for. I have some work to do anyway."

Silent, she watched him stalk away from her. She hadn't meant to be so harsh, but she didn't think it was fair of him to judge her about something he knew nothing about. He didn't have kids. Hell, he wasn't even married. He'd never lost a wife. He had no idea what her life was like.

"Come, Angel, baby," she called softly. "Let's go back inside and get to work."

Now that her mood had soured, she might as well take advantage of it and get started packing up the decorations. The ones around the cabin were easy because she had all of the original boxes for that stuff. But when she went to tackle the tree decorations, she realized she was going to need to take a trip into town to purchase a storage bin.

That was okay. She would grab something to eat while she was in town. Then she remembered Angel. She didn't want to leave the pup alone.

"Well, I guess I will just have to get my food to go, huh?" she said to the sleeping pup. "But first, a shower."

She showered and dressed. Then, she and Angel got into her car and headed into to town. She went to the hardware store for a storage tub. Since everyone stopped her so they could fawn over Angel, she quickly realized this shopping trip was going to take a little longer than planned.

When she went into the store, Angel rode in the shopping cart. Stella got two tubs to be on the safe side. After she took them to her car, she called in an order at the pub, then decided to pay Howie a visit while she waited for her order to be prepared.

"Well, hello," the man greeted them when they entered. "Look at this beautiful little angel." He came around the counter and knelt to lavish the pup with attention. "Perfect name."

"Thanks. I guess Caleb told you?"

"He did. Oh, she is just precious."

"I know." Stella grinned. "I love her already."

"How could you not with a face like that?"

Angel licked his face, making him laugh.

"So, what brings you into town today?" Howie asked, standing up again.

"I had to get some storage tubs to pack up all of the Christmas decorations."

"I guess that means you're still planning on leaving tomorrow?"

Emotion clogging her throat, she nodded.

"Ah, well. We'll miss you."

"I'll miss you, too," she admitted. "It's going to be very hard to leave this place. It's just wonderful here."

Although Howie nodded in agreement, she could tell there was something he wanted to say, but he didn't. She wondered if Caleb had told him about his suggestion that she extend her time here.

"I'm definitely coming back," she said. "I'm hoping to have my own house, but if not, I'm going to rent a place."

Howie smiled. "Vacation home or are you planning on relocating permanently?"

The question caught her off guard. She hadn't considered living here permanently; she'd only considered a house here as a vacation home. She'd never thought about living on the lake, but she supposed it could be a possibility. After all, Caleb lived in his cabin full time.

The thought of Caleb caused a pinching sensation in her chest. Being in a disagreement with him made her sad.

"I'm guessing from your silence that you hadn't considered a permanent move," Howie said.

Coming back to attention, she replied, "No, I hadn't. As much as I would love to live here, I don't think it's a good idea. At least not right now."

"Seems to me it's the perfect time. Fresh start and all that."

Goodness, what was it with these people pushing her to move here? Didn't they understand that she had a life back home? That she had children to consider?

"Did you make a fresh start after your wife died?" she snapped. "Did you move away from your family?"

"No, I didn't. I had this business to consider. For the record, my kids weren't living here when their mother got sick. Caleb was off in New York and Celia was in Concord."

"I'm sorry. That was uncalled for. I shouldn't have snapped at you like that."

The poor man hadn't meant any harm. He was only trying to be helpful, and here she was being bitchy.

"It's okay," Howie said. "I remember the stress of finding my way after Loretta passed. Pretty sure I snapped at everyone back then."

"Even so, I am sorry."

Howie nodded. "Apology accepted. I'm sorry for pressuring you about how to live your life. It's none of my business."

"It's okay." She checked the time. "My dinner order should be ready. I'll stop back in to say goodbye before I leave."

"I'll see you then."

Then she and Angel were on their way to the pub. Since she couldn't take the puppy inside, a server brought her order out to her. Stella thanked her and then practically ran back to her car. She couldn't wait to get back to the cabin, where no one would try to tell her what to do.

CHAPTER 32

Stella's phone beeped just as she took the last bite of her burger. It was a message from Caleb telling her he had to head to New York for an early morning meeting with his publisher. She offered to keep Boomer, but he said that wouldn't be necessary.

Hoping to catch him before he left, she went outside, but his truck was gone and his house was dark. She couldn't believe he'd left without saying goodbye.

She went inside, cleaned up her dinner mess, and fed Angel. Then she took the pup outside. While Angel sniffed around the yard in search of the perfect potty spot, Stella sat down on the back porch and looked out over the water.

Her phone rang, making her jump.

"Hey, Mom," June said when she answered. "I just wanted to let you know that we all got home okay and we've eaten dinner."

"Thank you. How was the drive back?"

"It was fine. Kind of sad. I don't think any of us were too excited to get back to real life, you know?"

"I do know. I'm not really looking forward to it, either."

"So, no word on a place for sale?"

"Not yet."

"Bummer. So, did you and Caleb enjoy a quiet dinner without all of us underfoot?"

Stella swallowed. "Uh, no. I spent the day packing up the decorations and he had to go to New York."

"Oh no! You're by yourself! We should have stayed another day."

"It's okay. Caleb's trip was a last-minute thing. He has an urgent meeting with his publisher in the morning."

"I hope everything is okay."

So did Stella, and she wasn't just talking about the book. Because she didn't want June to worry, she decided to keep her spat with Caleb to herself. That and she wasn't up for anymore advice from other people.

They got off the phone and Stella called for Angel. They went back inside and Stella turned on the TV for some background noise while she got to work disassembling the tree. Once all of the ornaments were packed away, she poured herself a glass of wine and settled down to watch a movie.

She couldn't focus on the story because her mind kept going back to her squabble with Caleb. His reaction puzzled her. While she knew her words were harsh, she really didn't see the reason for him to shut down like he did. And then to leave without even seeing her? Well, that was a bit childish on his part, if you asked her.

Maybe it was a good thing that she was leaving so soon after all. If he was going to give up on them that quickly, then maybe they were better off ending things before they got started. Thank goodness she hadn't allowed herself to get too attached.

Yes, it was time to go home. There was no need to extend her time here now. It was time for the fairy tale to end.

Feeling much better about her return home, she turned off the TV, took Angel out one last time, and then headed up to bed. There was plenty to do the following day before she left. To ensure she got a good's night sleep, she took one of her prescribed sleeping pills.

The next morning, Stella woke rested and ready to tackle the rest of her to-do list. She placed a call to Howie about having someone remove the tree for her. He also agreed to have someone pick up the boxes of the things she couldn't fit in her car and take them to the post office for her. Then, she stripped all the beds and bagged all of the bedding. She would wash everything when she got home.

After giving every surface a wipe-down, she stood with her hands on her hips as she surveyed the little cabin that had been her home the past six weeks. You couldn't tell now because all of her personal belongings were loaded up in the car.

"Thank you, dear cabin," she said aloud. "For everything."

And that was that. She went outside on the porch and took a deep, cleansing breath. Apparently, Caleb wasn't going to make it back in time to see her off. It was already almost two o'clock in the afternoon and she hadn't heard anything from him. He'd said he would be back by the afternoon since his meeting was in the early morning.

She hoped everything was okay. While she didn't know much about the writing and publishing process, she did know that, no matter the profession, it wasn't usually a good thing when an emergency meeting was called by your boss. Wasn't that essentially what the publishing company was for writers?

As Angel sniffed around the yard, Stella sent Caleb a quick text to tell him she was sorry that they'd missed each other and she was leaving. She waited a couple of minutes for a reply and when none came, she loaded Angel into the car. Once the pup was settled and she still hadn't received a reply, she started the car and headed into town, where she would stop by to say goodbye to Darlene and Howie as she'd promised.

To her surprise, Stella found herself more emotional than expected at telling Howie goodbye. And she really got choked up when she knelt down to hug Boomer, who was apparently staying with Howie while Caleb was gone. To make matters worse, Darlene entered the store and hugged Stella tightly when she saw her tears.

"Well, now," Darlene said. "You're acting like we're never going to see you again and that's just not true, right?"

"No, I will be back," Stella said. "Leaving is just hard."

Even more so when you weren't exactly sure where the relationship you were leaving behind stood.

"You'll be back before you know it," Howie said.

Stella nodded and after another round of hugs, she was back in her car and on her way home.

The trip was uneventful, even with little Angel in the car. She was a great traveler and slept the whole way. To Stella's surprise, Noah was waiting for her when she pulled into her driveway.

"What are you doing here?" she asked.

"I'm here to help you unload your car."

"Thank you."

Together they unloaded everything. Noah pointed out she was awfully quiet and asked if everything was okay. She told him she was tired. It wasn't the whole truth, but she wasn't up to rehashing her tiff with Caleb. The incident was too fresh yet.

Noah kissed her cheek and was off to his own home. Stella took Angel out in the small backyard, so she could get acquainted with her new home.

While Angel explored, Stella looked around her tiny back yard. She'd always been content with this little plot of land to call her own, but now it felt almost claustrophobic. The neighboring houses were practically on top of her. If it weren't for blinds and curtains, she would be able to see right into their windows.

Her phone rang and she saw it was Caleb calling. Biting her lip, she debated not answering but decided that wasn't the right thing to do. After all, it's not like he just blew her off for no reason. He had *work*. She couldn't really fault him for that.

"Hello?" she answered.

"Hey. Did you get home okay?"

"I did, thank you."

"I'm sorry I didn't make it back before you left. I only just got home myself a little while ago."

"It's okay. Is everything okay with your book?"

He sighed. "No, but I don't want to talk about it. I've been talking about it all day."

Well, okay then.

"It was weird pulling up and not seeing any lights next door," he said. "This place never used to feel lonely. Now it does."

Although she liked knowing that he missed her, she didn't comment. She wasn't sure what to say.

"How is Angel?" he asked.

"She's good. Slept the whole drive and now she's exploring her backyard."

"That's good. Boomer is going to miss her."

"She'll miss him, too."

Another awkward silence stretched between them. It was disorienting to be home and talking to Caleb on the phone, as if her two different worlds were colliding. It somehow felt unnatural.

"Well, I'll let you go get settled," Caleb said. "I'm sure you're tired."

"I am," she admitted.

"I'll talk to you later then?"

"Sure."

"Goodnight, Stella."

"Goodnight, Caleb."

And that was that. One disastrously awful phone conversation.

"Angel, come," she said. "It's bed time."

CHAPTER 33

The next morning was all about trying to settle back into her routine, while establishing one for Angel at the same time. Stella spent most of the day washing laundry and cleaning. The house had gotten stuffy and dusty while she was gone. Even though it was freezing outside, she opened a couple of windows in the hopes of fresh air chasing away the stuffiness weighing her down.

By lunch time, the cleaning was done and since her teeth were chattering, she closed the windows. It didn't take long for the walls to start closing in on her. She didn't understand how a bigger house could feel much more confining than a smaller cabin, but it did.

She fixed herself a sandwich for lunch and jotted down a grocery list while she ate. The thought of going to the chain grocery store was overwhelming, so she went online and placed a delivery order instead.

"Well, Angel," she said to the pup sitting at her feet. "This is it. I hope you're not too terribly disappointed with your new life."

Angel gave a little bark and wagged her tail. Stella couldn't help but smile. It was nice having someone else here. She couldn't imagine how much harder it would be to adjust if she'd been completely alone.

"Thank you," she told Angel. Then she gave her a little scrap of turkey.

After lunch, she and Angel went for a walk around the neighborhood. The exercise was good for both of them. Angel got her energy out sniffing everything she passed and Stella found the crisp air refreshing.

When they returned home, Stella was surprised to see June's car in the driveway. She and Angel barely made it inside before the kids came running.

"Angel! I missed you!"

"Hey, Angel! How are you?"

Laughing, Stella unhooked the excited dog's leash and watched as she chased the kids into the living room, where they proceeded to have a wrestling match.

"You would think they hadn't seen each other in years," June said, shaking her head. But she was smiling when she turned to her mother. "Hey. The kids wanted to visit. I hope that's okay."

"Oh, honey," Stella said as she hugged her. "Of course it's okay! You know you all are welcome here anytime. Have you eaten?"

"Yes, we had lunch before we came over."

"Okay. Good because I'm still waiting on my grocery delivery and I don't have much to offer." Stella laughed. "How about some tea?"

"Actually, I already have some steeping. I figured you might enjoy a cup after your walk. It's cold out there."

"It is, but Angel and I needed the exercise." Stella followed her daughter into the kitchen, where two mugs sat waiting next to the teapot. "Thank you for making the tea. You know me well."

Rolling her eyes, June said, "Of course I do. You're my mom." She sat down on a stool. "So, tell me. Is it really hard being back?"

Stella forced a smile. "It's an adjustment, but it's fine."

June's eyes narrowed. "What is it? What's wrong?"

"What makes you think anything is wrong?"

"Your eyes. They're … sad. You miss Caleb, don't you? You hate being here now. I knew it. You're going to move to that lake, aren't you?"

Flabbergasted, Stella held up a hand. "Whoa, June. Take it easy. Of course, I'm sad about leaving Evergreen Point. Weren't you sad when you left?"

"Well, yeah, but it's different for you. You left your boyfriend behind."

"Caleb isn't my boyfriend." She frowned. "At least, I don't think he is."

"I thought you two were together? And I figured after we all left, you would be *together*."

"Well, you thought wrong."

June's face fell. "He didn't make it back before you left."

Stella nodded.

"So, you didn't get a proper goodbye? What the hell is wrong with that man? I swear. Sometimes men can be so dense. Have you at least spoken to him since you got home?"

"Yes. He called last night. It was … awkward."

"Awkward? Why? You two get along so easily."

"We had a bit of a disagreement before he left."

"About what?"

Stella shook her head as she poured their tea. "Doesn't matter. He said something that upset me, and I guess I did the same. He clammed up and left."

"You mean you didn't talk about it?" June scoffed. "Men." Her face softened as she looked at Stella. "Do you think you will work it out?"

"I'm not sure about anything anymore," Stella admitted sadly.

June put her arm around her shoulders and squeezed. "I'm sorry, Mom. I'm sure you two will figure things out. I hope you do. You two are good together."

Startled by her daughter's admission, Stella took a sip of tea to try to cover up her surprise. June was the last person she expected to root for her and Caleb to make up.

"You were probably expecting a different reaction," June said. "I know I've been all over the place lately, and I'm sorry for that, but I hope you know that I *do* want you to be happy, Mom."

"Thank you, honey."

June grabbed her hand. "I mean it. I think you should talk to Caleb and try to straighten things out."

"Even if it means I could possibly end up moving to be with him?"

Flinching, June nodded. "Yes. I would hate to see you leave, but if that's what you need to do to find happiness, then I'll just have to deal with it."

Smiling, Stella said, "Well, Caleb and I did kind of talk about going back and forth, so I don't think I would be moving to Evergreen Point permanently."

Even though June tried to hide it, Stella saw the look of relief that flashed across her face. She didn't comment on it though. Instead, she suggested they go into the living room and join the kids, so they did.

June and the kids stayed for about an hour and a half. After they left, Stella took Angel outside again for another potty break. While she waited for the pup to do her business, she thought about June's encouragement to call Caleb. She knew avoiding the situation was beyond childish, but she wasn't sure she had the emotional capacity to deal with Caleb right now. She was tired. The past few days had been a roller coaster for her.

When Angel was finished, they went back inside and Stella put on some comfy clothes and got cozy on the sofa. She turned on the TV and got lost in a comforting re-run of one of her favorite old sitcoms.

CHAPTER 34

Two days went by and all she'd heard from Caleb was a text explaining that he was on a deadline to fix a problem with his manuscript so he would be MIA for a few days. She told herself that was good, since she didn't feel strong enough to deal with whatever was going on between them.

It was a lie, of course. She hated that things were still strained between them. But she had to respect his work and his need to focus. Given that emergency meeting, whatever was wrong with his manuscript must be pretty severe.

She decided to use her free time by focusing on the upcoming New Year's celebration. June and Will were hosting a party at their house and Stella always helped them prepare. She baked desserts and appetizers that could be made in advance. Then she went to their house to help decorate.

She couldn't believe the New Year was already upon them. If felt like just yesterday she was wrestling with her decision to go to Evergreen Point for the holidays.

"Okay," June said as she slid a tray into the oven. "I think we're good to go. Time to get dressed."

Stella went up to the guest room to change into her dress. They always dressed up for the party. She put on her make-up and pulled her hair up into a sophisticated twist. Then she went to check on the kids.

The kids generally stayed upstairs with a couple of babysitters and had their own little celebration before the ball drop. It was a way for the adults to relax and enjoy themselves downstairs without having to worry about their kids.

"Grandma, you look pretty!" Lizzie said when she saw Stella.

"Thank you. Are you excited to see your friends?"

"Yes!"

The doorbell rang downstairs, signaling the arrival of the sitters. They always showed up an hour before the party started. Will called up the stairs that he would answer the door, so Stella went to June's room to see if she needed any help with her dress or anything.

"Hey, Mom. I think I'm good. What do you think? I put on a little holiday weight."

Watching her daughter turn in a slow circle, Stella shook her head. "You look great! Holiday weight? Pfft. That dress looks amazing on you."

"Thanks." June glanced at the clock on her bedside table. "I guess I should get downstairs."

They went downstairs, passing the sitters on their way up. Will always got them settled with the kids, while Stella and June tended any last-minute duties in the kitchen.

"You guys look beautiful," Noah said.

"You're here early," June pointed out before kissing his cheek. "What? No date?"

"Nah. Just me this year."

"Well, that's kind of sad," June said.

"Hey, I've got the best date in the house." Noah draped his arm over Stella's shoulders.

Laughing, Stella shook her head. "Oh, no. Don't you dare use me as an excuse."

"Okay, fine. I didn't have anyone to bring. Are you happy now?"

June stuck out her tongue and Noah swatted at her. Sighing, Stella stepped between them, muttering about a mother's work never being done. June and Noah laughed.

"Seriously, though," Noah said. "Anything I can help with?"

"Um, can you make sure all the chairs have been moved from the garage and are positioned around the living and dining rooms?"

"I'm on it, sis."

Stella followed June into the kitchen to help her set up some of the food trays. The next thing she knew the party was well under way. She made the rounds, greeting everyone and making sure they had drinks and knew where to find the food. Once she was sure everyone was good to go, she got a glass of wine and went out onto the back porch to get some air.

She had to admit, it did feel good to be back in the swing of things. Sure, she still missed Dale terribly, but it was getting easier to interact with people with each passing day. This year was definitely better than last year. Dale's passing was no longer the elephant in the room.

"Hey," Noah said as he stepped outside. "What on earth are you doing out here?"

"I just needed some fresh air."

"You're missing your daily walks, aren't you?"

"Oh, Angel and I go for a couple of walks every day."

He shook his head. "No thanks. Too cold for that. Good for you though. Speaking of Angel, where is she?"

"I left her at home in the laundry room. She wasn't too happy about it, but I didn't want her under everyone's feet here. Plus, it's a little too crowded for her. She'd be scared to death."

Noah chuckled. "It's a little too crowded for me."

"Yeah. It's fun though."

"Sure. Have you spoken to Caleb?"

She shook her head. "He's been busy with his book. Some problem he had to rewrite or something. I'm not sure what all that entails, but I know from experience that when he's in writing mode, it's pointless trying to talk to him."

"Ah. Does he get snappy?"

"Oh, no. He just can't really focus on anything else. It's like talking to a zombie or something."

Noah laughed. "Well, then I guess it's good to leave him be. Let's get back inside. I can't feel my toes."

She followed him inside and they mingled with the guests. The night went by quickly with no drama, and before Stella knew it, it was already eleven o'clock. She went into the kitchen to help June begin setting out glasses for the champagne.

As they lined them up on the counter, she realized Noah was conspicuously absent. "Where is your brother?" she asked June.

"I don't know. I haven't seen him in a while. Leave it to him to skip out when there's work to be done."

"Oh, stop it. He helps you out every year. Which is exactly why it's odd that he's not here."

June shrugged. "Maybe he found himself a date after all."

"Wouldn't that be lovely?"

Stella had been patiently hoping and waiting for years for Noah to finally find someone and settle down. It didn't matter if they married or not; she just wanted to see her son happy. He hadn't been in a serious relationship in years.

Noah rushed into the kitchen just then. "Sorry I'm late. Here, Mom, let me take over for you."

"What are you talking about?" she asked as he plucked two flutes from her hands.

"Need any help?"

She whirled around at the sound of Caleb's voice. He was standing in the kitchen doorway dressed in a black suit that hugged his frame in the most delicious way. His dark hair was combed and gelled. Her body immediately responded with that familiar tingle underneath her skin and that ball of heat flaring in her lower belly.

"Caleb! What are you doing here?" she gasped.

"I wanted to talk to you and I figured it would be better in person."

She turned back to Noah. "You! I knew you were up to something!"

Noah shrugged. "You're welcome. Now go find a quiet place to talk. Go on. Shoo!"

As Stella crossed the kitchen, she heard June say, "Well done, brother."

CHAPTER 35

Caleb took Stella by the hand and led her down the hall. The second he touched her, it was like an electric shock coursing through her and awakening all of the nerves in her body.

"Upstairs," she said quietly, laughing when she saw his shocked face. "It's the only place we can be alone *to talk*."

She led him to the guest room and they barely made it inside before he had her in his arms and was kissing her. Kissing him back, she realized how much she'd missed him.

He pulled back and looked down into her eyes. "Hi," he said. "I missed you."

"I missed you, too. I can't believe you're here."

"The second I submitted my revised pages, I knew I had to see you, so I called Noah."

"You two love to conspire against me. First, Angel, and now this. I'm going to have to keep my eyes on you."

"Never against you, Stella. *For* you. We conspire for you."

Her heart melted a little bit. "Thank you."

"I'm sorry about the way we left things. I'm even sorrier about leaving and not making it back in time to say goodbye."

"You had work."

He shook his head. "I mean, I did, but I used it as an excuse. Because I wasn't ready to tell you the truth." He drew her hands up so that he could brush his lips along her knuckles. "I am now."

"Oh, God. You're not secretly married, are you?"

He laughed. "No. But I was. Married, I mean."

She thought back to what she'd said before, accusing him of not knowing what it was like to be married. Her stomach knotted.

"She left me, and I was blindsided. I'd be lying if I said I didn't still love her."

Stunned, Stella withdrew her hands from his. "*What?*"

"Hang on. Stay with me, Stella." He drew a shaky hand through his hair and blew out a breath. "It's true; I do still love her. She was my first love. We married young; we were only twenty. I was head over heels, fawning all over her all the time in love with her, which is why I was caught completely off guard when she ran off with my best friend." Dropping his gaze to his feet, he paused and licked his lips. She could see that this was difficult for him, so she refrained from saying anything. When his eyes met hers again, they were red-rimmed and glistening with tears. "We had a baby. A son. He-he died in his sleep when he was ten months old."

Stella gasped and covered her mouth with a hand.

Caleb swallowed hard, closing his eyes against a fresh wave of grief. Then he continued. "It was a horrible thing to go through, but I thought we got past it. I did everything right. At least, I thought I did. I catered to her every whim trying to help her with her grief and loss. I thought we were okay. Thought we were finally back on track. Until a year later when I came home and found her gone, leaving only a note in her place. She'd run off with my best friend."

"That's awful," she finally whispered.

"She apologized. Said she just couldn't do it anymore. That every time she looked at me, she saw Sam's face and it was too much. I get it. Grief ... it changes people. Sometimes in a good way, sometimes not."

"Do you still talk to her?"

"No. She and Landon moved to the west coast. Some place in Washington. She needed a new start, she said. She couldn't stay in New York anymore because it reminded her of Sam." He gave her a sad smile. "I'm happy for them. They're still together and Landon was able to give Megan whatever it was that she needed that I couldn't."

"Caleb, I'm so sorry. For having to go through that. For what I said to you."

"It's okay. You didn't know. How could you?"

She stepped forward to hug him, inhaling his familiar spicy scent as she did.

"So, you see," he said, holding her tight. "I do have a little experience with losing a wife. That's why I tried so hard to fight my feelings for you at first. I understood that you were going through a tough time and I didn't want to take advantage of you."

"And it brought up some of your own bad memories, I'm sure."

It made sense now. That night he'd suddenly left, and then again when she'd essentially hit on him. He was trying to be a gentleman and battling his own emotions at the same time. She knew a thing or two about trying to move on when you still loved someone else.

"I'm sorry I didn't tell you sooner," he said. "You were already dealing with so much. I didn't want to add to your distress."

Tipping her head back to look him in the face, she said, "It's okay. I'm sorry for acting the way I did. Saying the things I did."

He leaned down and touched his forehead to hers. "So, what do you say? Do you think we can give this thing between us a go? For real this time? Help each other move on from our first loves?"

Downstairs, the partygoers began to count down.

"I would love to," Stella said, standing up on her toes to press her lips to his.

Downstairs everyone yelled 'Happy New Year!' and began cheering.

"Happy New Year, Stella."

"Happy New Year, Caleb."

They returned downstairs and Stella introduced him to her friends. To her surprise, no one seemed critical of her being with him. Considering he wouldn't let go of her hand, there was no denying they were a couple now.

"Caleb," June said, engulfing him in a giant hug. "It's wonderful to see you again. I'm so happy to see you together. I haven't seen Mom this happy in a while. Thank you for that."

"Wait a minute," one of June's friends suddenly came over to them. "I know why you look so familiar. You're C.J. Abrahams! Oh, my gosh! I love your books!"

The guests began to crowd around them, all of them asking questions about his new book, and Stella found herself pushed away from Caleb's side. He immediately reached through the crowd and pulled her back.

June and Will got their excited guests under control and Stella and Caleb made a run for it. They were about to get into Stella's car when Noah came running outside.

"Hang on!" he yelled, waving a bottle over his head. When he got to the car, he said, "Wow. Caleb, I knew you were a famous author, but holy shit, you're a famous author!"

Caleb laughed and Stella chastised him for language.

"Sorry, Mom. It's the bubbles. I swear they go straight to my head. Oh! Speaking of bubbles, here. You two can't celebrate without some champagne. I meant celebrate the book. Oh, geez. Anyway, Happy New Year!"

Stella couldn't contain her own laughter as they watched Noah run back into the house.

"Well, I hope he has someone to drive him home," Caleb said.

"June will see to it."

The drive to Stella's house was quiet, yet intense. They were both caught up in their own thoughts and fears. The closer they got to the house, the more Stella's stomach began to churn. She'd been so caught up in the moment that she hadn't stopped to think that she was bringing a man home to the house she'd shared with her husband. And not just the house, *the bed*.

When she pulled into the driveway, she stared at the house looming in front of her. It was suddenly difficult for her to catch her breath.

"Hey, I have an idea," Caleb said. "Let's go inside and you can pack a bag while I get Angel. Then we can go to my hotel."

She turned to him in surprise. "You got a hotel room?"

"Well, I didn't want to be presumptuous." He grinned. "And I figured it might be a good idea to have options. You know, in case you needed them."

"You're perfect, you know that?" she said before kissing his cheek.

"Whoa, now. Don't go setting high expectations like that. I can't handle that level of pressure."

"Oh, I think you'll handle it just fine."

His eyes twinkled with delight. "Oh, you do, do you?"

"Yes, I do. Now, let's go get my stuff so we get back to your hotel and pop the cork on this bottle and celebrate."

CHAPTER 36

The next morning, Stella and Caleb ordered room service for a light breakfast. Stella always met up with the family for a late brunch on New Year's Day. They rushed to her house so she could get the breakfast casserole in the oven.

When everyone arrived, they greeted Caleb as if he was already a part of the family, which gave Stella mixed emotions. She could tell it was the same for June.

"You okay?" she asked June quietly.

"Yes. No. Yes. It's weird."

"I know what you mean. I freaked out last night when we got here. That's why we ended up back at Caleb's hotel room."

"You didn't stay here?"

Stella shook her head. "I wasn't ready for that. Caleb understood." She gave June's arm a gentle squeeze. "He's very understanding about the situation, so if you ever feel uncomfortable, say something. He doesn't want it to feel like he's trying to take over."

June nodded. "That's nice. He really is a great guy."

"He is. Just give him a chance."

The kids asked Caleb where Boomer was, and he told them he was at home. Seeing their disappointment, he promised to bring him for a visit soon.

The meal went pleasantly. Afterwards, the kids settled in the living room for a movie, while the adults hung out in the kitchen. Everyone happily pitched in with the clean-up then gathered around the table once more. This time with coffee and tea.

They chatted, getting to know Caleb a little better and vice versa. The whole time Stella sat back and watched with a smile on her face. Seeing her family now, she wondered what she was so worried about before. Caleb seemed to fit right in. So much so, she knew in her heart that Dale would approve. In fact, she was willing to bet that if Dale were still here and they'd gone to Evergreen Point together, he and Caleb would have been fast friends.

"Mom?"

She jerked in her chair at the sound of Noah's voice. "Sorry. I was lost in thought. What?"

"I said you should probably check your email."

"My email? Why?"

Her son rolled his eyes. "Just do it."

"Fine." She brought up her email app on her phone and checked her inbox. When she saw Celia's name she gasped. "Is this what I think it is?"

"What is it?" June asked.

Stella clicked the button and there it was. A listing for a house on Evergreen Lake. She held her phone out so Caleb could see it.

"That's the Mundy's place about six houses down from mine," he said. "It's a great house. They've only owned it for about four years. I'm surprised they're selling."

"Any issues? Is the price reasonable?"

He looked over the details. "No issues that I'm aware of. They've taken care of it. And that price is lower than expected."

"Okay." Stella typed a reply and then looked at her family. "I just made an offer. I hope that's okay."

"Of course it's okay!" June said.

"Absolutely," Noah said. "But can we at least see the pictures of it now?"

She frowned. "She sent it to you, too. Didn't you look at it?"

He shook his head. "No, this is your thing. I didn't want to spoil it."

As they passed the two phones around so everyone could look at the pictures, Caleb slipped away. Stella noticed, but didn't say anything. When he came back, he explained that the listing hadn't officially hit the realtor sites yet, and that Celia had told the Mundy's about a possible buyer. Celia also added that the Mundy's were getting divorced and looking to unload the house, fully furnished, as quickly as possible.

"That's good, right?" Stella asked.

"Well, it's not so good for the Mundy's," Noah said. "I mean, it's the end of their marriage."

"Shut up, Noah!" June exclaimed. "No one cares about the Mundy's." Then she looked at Caleb. "I mean …"

Caleb smiled. "It's okay. I didn't know them that well. They kept to themselves. I just helped look after the house as needed."

"Oh, okay." June said. "I don't mean to sound so harsh."

"You're excited," Caleb said. "As you should be. This is very exciting."

June's gaze met Stella's and she smiled.

Stella's phone beeped and she saw the official offer paperwork was ready for her to sign.

"Man, your sister doesn't waste any time," she said.

"No, she doesn't."

Two hours later it was official: Stella was the owner of a lake house in Evergreen Point.

"This calls for more champagne!" Noah said, jumping up to go through the fridge.

"Didn't you have enough last night?" Will asked. "Or do you not remember?"

"How could he forget dancing around our backyard in nothing but his boxers in twenty-eight-degree weather?" June asked incredulously.

Noah froze, his cheeks going scarlet. "That did *not* happen."

"Oh, I assure you, it absolutely *did* happen." June waggled her eyebrows dramatically. "*And* I have pictures to prove it, brother of mine."

"Shit."

"Noah!" Stella said before turning to her daughter. "You seriously have pictures?"

"*Mom!*" Noah cried. "June, don't you dare."

"How about we all get back to celebrating your mother's new lake house?" Caleb suggested, winking at Noah.

"Oh, right," Stella said. "I don't think I have any champagne though."

225

"No worries," Noah said from inside the fridge. "Here's a bottle of Rosé. That will work."

"Ew, no," Will said. "I'm not drinking pink wine. Gross."

"Hey, we're equal opportunity drinkers around here, mister."

"No, Noah," June said laughing. "That's *you*!"

As the table erupted in laughter and teasing, Stella reached down and squeezed Caleb's hand. He turned, smiled, and squeezed back before kissing her cheek.

She asked, "Are you sure you still want to be a part of this wacky family?"

"Absolutely."

EPILOGUE

Calling out to Boomer and Angel, Stella started the trek back to the house. It was almost time for her family to arrive. It had been almost a year since she'd bought her house in Evergreen Point and now, she and her family were going to experience their first Christmas in it.

Stella had spent two days decorating the five-bedroom house. Caleb said it looked like an elf had thrown up Christmas all over the place. Sure, she may have gone a little bit overboard, but that was okay. After all, they *were* in Evergreen Point. And sure, it wasn't technically their *first* Christmas in Evergreen Point, but it definitely wasn't going to be their last. So, yes, Stella may have gone to extremes with the decorations but she was so excited she didn't care.

She and Caleb split their time between here and her house in Massachusetts. Over the summer they spent most of their free time here with her family visiting every weekend they could. They were getting their money's worth out of this place for sure.

While Stella loved every second her family spent here, she secretly counted down the days until Christmas. This time of year would always be special to her and she couldn't wait to continue to share the magic of Christmas in Evergreen Point with her family year after year.

When she got back to the house, Noah was already there and waiting for her with a steaming mug of tea.

"Hello, dear," Stella said, hugging him. "Where's everyone else?"

"You know June had to stop by Darlene's. She's so addicted to her Snickerdoodle cookies I'm surprised she hasn't gained fifty pounds already."

"Be nice to your sister. Thank you for the tea, by the way."

"You're welcome. Where's Caleb?"

"At his cabin."

Caleb had kept his cabin so he would have a quiet place to write. He treated it more like an office now, but Stella had to admit that having a second house did come in handy when they wanted some quiet time alone.

"How's the new book coming along?" Noah asked.

"Okay, I guess. He doesn't talk about it much until it's nearly completed. Something about not wanting unsolicited suggestions or something like that."

Noah emphatically rolled his eyes. "Writers."

Stella laughed. "I know."

June and her family entered the house then, bringing all of their excitement with them. Since they visited the house frequently, there wasn't much to unpack, just the Christmas presents and a few bags. Everyone had their own wardrobes and toiletries and such stashed here.

"Hello, Mom," June finally hugged her. "Is Caleb at his cabin?"

"Yes. I should text him and tell him you're here."

"Don't you dare bother him," June said. "There's no need to distract him from his work."

"Can you tell she's anxious for his new book to come out?" Will said.

"Well, there's nothing wrong with that," Stella said.

She loved how supportive June was of Caleb's work and the relationship they'd developed surrounding it.

"Actually, sis, it is kind of weird the way you have your mother's boyfriend on a pedestal," Noah teased.

"At least I read his books."

"Hey! I read his books."

Stella and Will shared a look as the siblings began to argue about what book of Caleb's that Noah had last read.

The kids had abandoned them and were playing with the dogs in the living room.

Stella sat back and basked in the sound of good-natured arguing and joyous laughter. She loved having her family here.

"Hey, hey!" Caleb called as he came into the house.

The dogs barked and ran to greet him with the children on their heels. Caleb petted the dogs and hugged the kids before coming to kiss Stella on the cheek.

"Hey," he said.

"Hey," she replied.

Caleb straightened and then turned his attention to the rest of the adults, asking about the drive. The men shook hands and June hugged him as they chatted about their trip. Pretty soon the talk turned to the upcoming Christmas Eve celebration in town. Stella wasn't sure who was more excited this year, the kids or the adults.

Everyone was looking forward to another magical Christmas in Evergreen Point.

Author's Note

Thank you for reading Christmas in Evergreen Point! I hope you enjoyed Stella's story. Please, don't forget to leave a review!

Acknowledgements

I would like to thank Katie, April, and Natalie (welcome to the team!) for your time, suggestions, and edits. This book would not have been possible without your support. You guys rock!

As always, I would like to send a big shout-out to my family for not only supporting me and my dream, but also for putting up with my moodiness and quirks, especially during editing and formatting time. I know I can be a PITA, but none of this would be possible without you.

And of course, READERS! This book exists because of you. Thank you so much for sticking with me and supporting my work. You guys are the reason I do this. Thank you for taking the time out of your busy lives to escape into my imaginary worlds with me.

About the Author

Angela Flowers lives in Virginia with her husband, two sons, and two rambunctious dogs. In addition to writing, she also enjoys reading, binging TV shows, and spending time at home with her family.

Born a lover of words and stories, she began reading at an early age and then crafting her own stories as soon as she could write. She later attended Christopher Newport University, where she earned a B.A. in English with a concentration in Creative Writing.

Angela is a voracious reader who will read just about any genre. Romance, historical fiction, mysteries, thrillers…as long as the story is good, she will read it.

Connect

angelaflowersbooks.com

Facebook, Instagram, & Threads: @aflowersauthor

Other Books

Silver Linings Romance Series:
Silver Linings
Catch Perfect
Masquerade
Fool's Paradise
For Better, For Worse
Always and Forever

Standalone Romance:
Just Alex
The Change Up